I0699462

It App -ened One Night

Victoria Hamel

PB & A Publishing

PB & A Publishing supports the copyrights of human authors. Thank you for reading an authorized edition of this book and for complying with the copyright laws by not reproducing, scanning, or distributing any part of it in any form without written permission from the author. You are supporting writers. For more copyright information, please write to victoria@victoriahamelauthor.com

This is a work of fiction. Names, characters, businesses, places, events, locales, and incidents are either the products of the author's imagination or used in a fictitious manner. Any resemblance to actual persons, living or dead, or actual events is purely coincidental. Cover design by Getcovers.com.

eBook Edition ISBN- 979-8-9897583-6-4

Paperback ISBN-13: 979-8-9897583-7-1

Contents

Also By Victoria Hamel

♥

Book One in the Marley Creek Romance Series; *No Gouda Without You*

Get your copy of book one here:
https://a.co/d/jeeF06E

Book Two in the Marley Creek Romance Series: *Too Kölsch For Comfort*

**Get your copy of book two here:
https://a.co/d/0avDaHZ**

**Book Three in the Marley Creek Romance Series:
*Is This Love Fur Real?***

Get your copy here: https://a.co/d/fEIOZJx

Book Four in the Marley Creek Romance Series: *It App-ened One Night*

Get your copy here: https://a.co/d/5qpVaaj

**Book Five in the Marley Creek Romance Series:
*Your Mr. Brightside***

**Pre-order your copy here:
https://a.co/d/h1TWrEV**

Sign up for Victoria's free newsletter for sneak peeks, special offers and more by visiting her website https://victoriahamelauthor.com

About the Author

♥

Victoria's love of writing began in grade school where she won an award for a Mother's Day essay. She spent the better part of her childhood with her head in a book. In high school, she wrote love stories for her friends in which they'd meet their favorite bands or the movie star they had a crush on. Suffice it to say, Victoria was writing fan fiction before fan fiction was a thing. After spending many years starting and stopping writing in various genres, Victoria returned to her high school roots and began writing romance.

Victoria Hamel lives in the Chicago area with her husband, three college-age kids and Bowie the dog. She has run three marathons and based on that experience; she feels qualified to say that reviewing her manuscript for errors was a more arduous task than literally running a marathon. She is a member of the Chicago North Romance Writers Group as well as Contemporary Romance Writers. When she isn't writing, Victoria volunteers for local democrat candidates, watches K-Dramas, or can be found blogging on her blog *First of All...*

You can find the other books in the Marley Creek Romance series here or via any independent bookstore:

https://www.amazon.com/stores/author/B0CSBGDRFQ

Subscribe to my newsletter for exclusive bonus scenes, ARC opportunities, and all the news!

Acknowledgements

♥

This book would not exist if I hadn't started following Maria Secoy's live videos on Facebook. Thanks to Maria and her writer-to-author program, I am now a publishing my fourth book! If you've spent years wanting to write a book, check out All Write Well www.allwritewell.comit may be just what you need to finish that book!

Thanks so much to my husband Tom for being my hype man! Even though he doesn't get romance books, he's still happy to be a sounding board and share my book news with everyone he meets.

Thanks to the Chicago North Romance Writers Group for critiques. Thank you to Jen at https://jenreadsromance.com for an amazing brainstorming session. Thank you to Bryn Donovan for editing this book. Thank you to Ashley Lewis for your excellent proofreading! https://allthingsgeekygirl.com

Thanks to my ARC Readers and my newsletter subscribers! Your support is everything!

Thank you to all the readers! I am so grateful for your time. There are so many books out there and you chose this one!

Chapter One

♥

Susan

Susan Brown shifted in the plastic seat next to her mom's wheelchair. She crossed her legs, regretting she'd worn shorts today. It was the first week of October, and it was eighty-six degrees outside. However, here in the waiting room, it was sweater weather. She should finally get around to unpacking her fall clothes. Maybe that would bring on some seasonal temperatures.

Susan sighed, already missing Illinois State. She'd always loved the fall there. The campus had the quintessential college quad with soaring trees and aged brick buildings. This was the first fall in twenty years she wouldn't be there to watch the leaves change and fall to the ground. Her chest tightened. Instead, she was at St. Stanislaus Hospital with her mom.

"Suzy, can you stop fidgeting?"

Susan clenched her jaw. Even though she was nearly forty, her mother still acted like she was sixteen. She uncrossed her legs and turned toward her mom. She needed to remember to be patient with her. A doctor didn't need to tell her that her mom was still in a lot of pain. But was it the pain? Her mom had always been quick to tell her to stop doing things her entire life. That was the reason she rarely came home since she left for college.

"It's freezing in here."

"That's why I have my sweater."

Susan frowned. She'd foolishly hoped her mom would be happy to have her around. Then again, her mom thought she was taking family leave. Her stomach filled with acid. Her mom didn't know that Susan, along with the entire applied education department, had been let go over the summer.

The first night at the hospital, her mother had asked if she'd be able to stay a few days or if she had to go back to work. The stress of seeing the woman who'd always been such a stern and strong parent cocooned in a hospital bed with IVs had gotten to her. She'd told her mother she'd stay with her until she could get back on her feet. Dorothy had assumed Susan had family leave to take, and Susan hadn't said otherwise.

Of course, she'd tell her mom about her new situation, she just wanted to wait until Dorothy was further on in her recovery. Susan knew how her mom would start nagging her about looking for a job and worrying that Susan would struggle to find new employment. She wouldn't admit it out loud, but a small part of her clung to the idea that her career wasn't dead as long as her mom didn't know about her getting let go.

Susan pulled a pack of gum out of her pocket. "Do you want a piece?"

Dorothy looked away from the local TV station's morning show and toward her daughter. She pursed her thin lips and tapped her fingers on the arm of her wheelchair. "What I'd like is a cigarette."

"Those days are over for you." Susan remembered begging her mom to quit smoking when she was a kid, but it hadn't been until six weeks ago that she'd finally put the cigarettes down. "Did you take your Bupropion?"

Dorothy scoffed. "You know I did. You watched me take a handful of pills this morning."

A door opened and a female voice said, "Dorothy Brown, you can come back now."

A phlebotomist wearing pink scrubs stood at the door and waited. Susan got up and pushed her mom into the exam room. As soon as she began hunting for a vein in Susan's mom's bruised arm, Susan averted her eyes and pulled out her phone. Even though she knew by now that this part of the hospital had almost no internet service, she'd rather watch her email try to load than see her mom getting stuck. Susan shuddered.

Her mother snorted. "Wimp."

Susan opened her mouth to respond, then decided against it. Her mother had always been Susan's harshest critic, and neither age nor her broken hip had mellowed her.

Snap. The phlebotomist removed the rubber tourniquet from Dorothy's arm. "We're all done. Your doctor should have the results in a day or two. Do you have the app?"

Dorothy shook her head. "I don't do apps." Then she pointed at her daughter. "She's got my app on her phone."

The technician turned to Susan. "You'll get a notification when the results are in."

"Thanks so much."

Susan got behind her mom's wheelchair and pushed her out of the lab.

Once they were in the hallway, Dorothy chided her. "Why were you thanking her? You weren't the one who had to get stuck again. What if it hurt like the dickens?"

Susan spoke in the tone she used when she'd been student teaching kindergarten years ago. "Don't you want to be nicer to me? Remember, I'm the one pushing your chariot."

"You're here now, but I know you are counting down the minutes till you can leave tonight."

She's not wrong about that. "I'll only be gone a few hours. Zaina's pregnant. We won't be out all night." Susan shook her head thinking about how long it had been since she'd been to a concert with her best friend from high school.

Susan stopped at the revolving door that marked the hospital's entrance. She put the brake on and walked around to face her mother. Dorothy's chin-length bob was gray. Her brown eyes were faded now, and the lines around her lips that had just been sprouting when Susan had last lived at home were tunnel deep.

"I'm going to get the car. You stay here."

"Where would I go, Suzy?"

Susan shrugged. "Who knows? Maybe a handsome doctor is about to sweep you off your feet?"

Dorothy made a pfft sound and tapped her middle finger against her thumb as if it would summon a cigarette.

Susan took her mother's lack of a retort as a win and went to get her SUV. She got her mom in the car, drove forty minutes home, and got her mom back out of the car and into the house. She helped her get to the bathroom and then made lunch. After all that was done, her mom took her pain medication. Susan loaded the dishwasher, walked down to the mailbox and got the mail—all medical bills—and started a load of laundry.

Finally, she had a moment to herself. She plopped down on the couch and put in her earbuds. She hit shuffle and closed her eyes. In just a few hours, she'd be seeing singer/songwriter Eliza Fitzsimmons from the tenth row. For the first time since she'd moved back home last month, she was going to have a night to herself.

Thank goodness she'd been able to find a caretaker via the local Marley Creek community page, and the fact her mom was willing to let a stranger come into her house and sit with her? That was a near miracle. Susan had been listening to Eliza Fitzsimmons since her first album came out. Eliza was the only musician she'd pay more than face value for tickets. Plus, she'd barely gotten to see Zaina since she'd gotten into town. A thrill ran through her, and she wiggled her toes, which reminded her she hadn't had a pedicure for a couple of months.

Susan doubted her mother had any nail polish remover lying around, so strappy heels were not going to be part of her outfit tonight. Even if the temperatures were unseasonably high, it was October in the Midwest, boots it would be. She set an alarm on her phone and fell asleep thinking about whether to straighten her hair for the show.

Before the alarm could go off, Susan phone vibrated her awake. She'd missed a call from Zaina. Susan put her phone down and closed her eyes again, she had ten more minutes before she needed to wake up. A minute later, her text notification went off, stirring her awake.

ZAINA: Please don't kill me!

Susan clicked on Zaina's contact and called her. Whatever was going on, it'd be faster to talk it out instead of trying to text. Zaina picked up on the first ring.

"I'm so sorry! This is the worst timing! I feel so bad!"

Susan's breath caught in her throat. "What's going on? Are you okay? How's the baby? Is it Jasper?"

"I just got home from the doctor. I'm not sure if I'm okay. I hope baby girl is okay and Jasper is a wreck!"

Susan's chest tightened. "Whatever's going on, I'm here for you! I'm not going to kill you."

"I know. You're the nicest. I mean, look at all you are doing for your mom, and well, she can be a real pain."

"Tell me about it. Now, back to you. What's going on?"

"Hopefully it's no big deal. I'm sure the doctor is overreacting. But when I woke up this morning, I noticed that my ankles were totally cankles. I mentioned it to the doctor, and for the record, it wasn't my usual, Dr. Kim, it was Dr. Donovan. He wasn't super concerned until they took my blood pressure, and it was higher than it's ever been during this whole pregnancy. The only thing I have going for me is that there isn't protein in my pee."

"Okay, what does that all mean?"

"Dr. Donovan says there's a small chance I could be developing pre-eclampsia, so I need to go on bed rest for now. I have a follow-up appointment next week, provided I don't have any headaches before then. I was really looking forward to seeing Eliza and hanging out with you! You know I love that song 'Over and Done, Or?'"

Susan put her head in her hands. Not only did one of her oldest friends have a pregnancy complication, now Susan wouldn't be going to the concert. She needed a night out so badly! She clenched her jaw to stop herself from letting out a yell of frustration.

"It's not your fault. Obviously, I understand. It's only a concert. We can go to one another time. Just think—a few months from now, I'm sure you'll be ready for a night out away from the baby."

"This sucks! I feel so bad doing this to you. You should still go."

"Who could I get to go with me? The concert is in a few hours." Going alone sounded somehow even more depressing than not going at all.

"Listen, I talked to Jasper about it, and he told me there is a new app for concerts. It's called Concert Buddy. If you have a ticket for a concert, you can sell it on the app and only people who are vetted can purchase the ticket."

"They vet people?" Susan asked.

"Yep. They make sure you don't get stuck next to some creep. You can even message before the concert so when you get to your seats you don't feel so awkward. Plus, you paid a ton for those tickets. Why should they go to waste?"

Susan frowned. Maybe this Concert Buddy app wasn't a terrible idea. "Does Jasper know anyone who used the app, or did he just hear about it?"

"Jax, his best bartender. They used it a few months ago and made such a good connection at the concert that now they've hung out with the person a few times."

"That's good to know."

"What have you got to lose?"

Susan ran a hand through her wavy dark brown hair. "My life? Or worse, the last tiny shreds of my dignity?"

Zaina chuckled. "You have plenty of dignity. You've never gone viral."

"That's true!" Susan said, remembering how Zaina and Jasper's video from the Frosty 5K that winter had made them Instagram stars for a few weeks.

"I'll send you an invite to the app. I downloaded it on the way home from the doctor."

"I can't believe you were thinking about me right after you found out you needed to go on bed rest. That's really sweet of you."

"I can't lie—part of the reason I downloaded the app, and everything was that I needed the distraction. If I think too hard about having pre-eclampsia and what that might mean, I can't even breathe."

"Oh, honey, it's going to be okay. You're doing exactly what the doctor wants you to do. Plus, you've got Jasper, your mom, and a ton of great friends. Baby girl is still kicking up a storm, right?" Susan could picture her tiny friend rubbing her enormous belly.

Zaina sniffed into the phone. "Now you are making me cry."

"I wish I could reach through the phone and give you a hug."

"I wish I could hug you right back," Zaina said.

"Would it help you to stay distracted if I give this app a try and keep you updated on my adventures at the concert?" Susan asked.

"That would be so helpful! You don't even know."

"Send me that invite now, then!" Susan said.

"Thank you so much. You are the best!"

"Now you keep your feet elevated, and I'll let you know if someone takes the ticket!"

"I have a good feeling about this. Text me as much as you can!"

"Bye, Zaina."

Susan ended the call. What has she gotten herself into?

Chapter Two

♥

Donnie

Donnie Larson hummed along with a song from the latest Eliza Fitzsimmons's release. Donnie had two favorite times of the day: three a.m., when he fed his sourdough starter and began his day at Books and Breads, and three p.m., when he closed the bakery for two hours and took a nap. He put on his hairnet, covering his short gray hair, and then donned his beard net, covering his auburn and gray full beard. When he'd participated in No-Shave November, aka Movember, a few years ago, he'd never thought he'd keep his beard, let alone allow it to grow several more inches.

He walked into his cooler and retrieved the heavy container of dough that had been resting overnight. Donnie flipped it over onto his stainless-steel worktable and divided it into a half-dozen loves. Each day he had at least four loaves for sale and used two for the daily sandwich offerings. On the shelf was his lame, a doubled sided blade for slicing the top of the sourdough loaves before baking. He slashed three cuts atop each round and oval boule and put them in the oven. As always, once the bread was baking, he fed his starter by adding water and flour to it.

He'd started making sourdough bread back when Sebastian was a baby. It was hard to believe it had been nearly sixteen years since he'd watched a public television TV show all about baking bread. Maggie had gone back to work, and Donnie had been unemployed, so he'd taken over as the primary caregiver for baby Sebastian. When it was time for the two a.m. feeding, Donnie would watch the "Breaking Bread" series. Learning sourdough was possible because of wild yeast in the air around us, fascinated him. Knowing all you needed to make it was flour, water, and time appealed to both him and Maggie, since they always had more bills left over after they used up her paycheck. Donnie's heart clenched. They'd been so happy early in their marriage.

He could still hear the lilt of Maggie's laugh when he told her he'd named his starter. She thought it was the silliest thing she'd ever heard. Who named yeast? He called that starter "June," and from then on, Maggie had joked her husband had a girlfriend on the side that he took care of every day. Donnie's eyes stung and he quickly wiped them, reliving those early days still got to him.

His phone shuffled to the next song on his playlist. The opening chords of "How Can You Be Gone?" began to play, and his heart ached. It had been nearly ten years since he'd last heard Maggie's voice and felt her touch, but this song always brought her back. As Eliza Fitzsimmons belted out the refrain, her voice almost became a wail, and Donnie sang along with her.

Before Maggie had died, he'd never understood bittersweet as an emotion. As a baker, he was well-versed in the chocolate version. These days, when memories of Maggie surfaced, he was happy to have her back in his mind. Over the last few years, he'd stopped thinking, *if only*. If only he'd insisted on driving her to work that day, then maybe she wouldn't have gotten into the accident. Now, it was rare for it to hurt when he saw her smile on their son's face.

The early morning hours rolled on and the bakery cases filled with donuts, pastries, rolls, quiches of the day, and his world-famous sourdough breakfast sandwiches. Well, world-famous was stretching it; more like local-famous. Books and Breads was located just around the corner from the Marley Creek Train Station. He knew without the commuter train he would have gone out of business ages ago. Another legacy of Maggie's; she'd been the one to notice when the space was up for lease, and later, it had been thanks to her insurance policy that he'd been able to buy the building.

The alarm went off on his phone. He turned it off and made a call to his son.

Ring.

Ring.

"I'm up." Sebastian said.

"Good morning, Buddy. Are you ready to have a great day at school?"

"Yes, sure, whatever."

"Text me when you get on the bus, so I know you caught it."

"Bye, Dad."

"I love you."

The call ended. Donnie sighed. He missed the days when his son had been not only happy to talk with him but had also said *I love you* back. His shoulders slumped, and he walked a little slower to the front door. He unlocked the door and flipped the sign to open.

***

By the time three p.m. rolled around, Donnie's knee was throbbing. He sat down at a table in the front of his store with an ice pack on it. The pain was cutting into his nap time. His part-time bookshop employee would be in at five tonight, so he had the evening to himself. Maybe Sebastian would want to go over to Jesse's Pub for dinner tonight. It was half-off wing night, after all. He unlocked his phone and called his son, but it went to voicemail. It wasn't like Sebastian to ignore his father's calls. Then again, he was fifteen. Donnie sent a quick text message.

> DONNIE: Want to go to Jesse's tonight? It's wings night.

He sent off the text and adjusted the ice pack on his knee. Hearing a knock on the door, Donnie looked up to see his friend Ethan waving. Donnie braced himself and stood up, wincing. He made his way over to the door and unlocked it.

"Hey, what's up?"

"Not much. I've got some time before I have to catch the train into the city for class tonight, so I thought I'd check up on you. It's been a minute."

"I don't think I've seen you since the August book club." Donnie said. He pulled out a chair for his young friend. "Can I get you something to drink?"

Ethan sat down. His dark brown hair was the same shade that Donnie's was back when he was in his early twenties. It was hard for Donnie to believe he was already in his mid-forties. Then his knee twinged, and he was well aware of his age.

"Any chance I can get a half-caff Americano?" Ethan asked.

"I have one brownie left. Want that with your coffee?"

Ethan patted his flat stomach. "No thanks. Got to keep myself in tiptop shape for Mable."

Donnie's lips made a straight line. "Dude, I'm pretty sure Mable loves you for more than your abs."

Ethan's brown eyes sparkled, and he broke out in a huge grin. "You're not wrong. She's the best."

Donnie put a to-go cup under the stream of espresso. Once it was done, he added hot water to finish the Americano. He put a lid on the cup. In his personal coffee cup, he poured a few ounces of brewed coffee. He walked out to the table where Ethan was sitting and set down their drinks.

"So, what's new? Are you going to the Eliza Fitzsimmons concert tonight?" Ethan asked.

"Nah."

"But I thought you were going to go? Didn't you say she hardly ever tours?"

"I did say that. I even asked Sebastian if he'd go with me. He grew up listening to her whenever he was in the car with me. I thought it would be a nice father/son bonding night."

"Let me guess: he has no interest." Ethan said.

"You guessed right. I don't know what I was thinking. I've forgotten what it's like to be a teenage boy. Of course he didn't want to go."

Ethan sipped his coffee. Donnie put the ice pack on his knee and leaned back, resting the coffee mug on his moderately rounded belly. Ethan frowned at his friend.

"You look sad. Everything okay?"

"I'm all right...just tired, I think." Donnie said.

"You should go to the concert. You need to get out."

"Are you going to skip class and go with me? Donnie asked.

Ethan crossed his arms and blew out his breath. "This accelerated teaching program is kicking my ass. I can't miss an in-person class."

Donnie ran a hand through his gray hair. "I'm so proud of you."

Ethan's cheeks reddened. "That means a lot, coming from you. You're like the older brother I never had."

Donnie chuckled. "Don't let your brother Sean hear you say that."

Ethan pursed his lips. "Good point. You're like the supportive uncle I never had."

Donnie smiled. "Better."

"As the favorite nephew you never had, I'm telling you to go to the concert."

Donnie took a sip of his coffee. He did love Eliza Fitzsimmons's music. It had been a constant source of comfort and joy throughout his adult life. She hadn't gone on tour in years, and the last time she'd come to Chicago had been right after Maggie had died.

"Maybe, I should go, but I'm sure it's sold out. And it's weird to go to a concert alone. Besides, I'm probably going to go to dinner with Sebastian."

Ethan was on his phone scrolling. "One sec."

Donnie's phone vibrated on the table. "That's him now."

"Bastian's calling?" Ethan asked while he continued looking at his phone.

"It's a text. Let me see what's up." Donnie pulled his reading glasses out of his shirt pocket and put them on.

> SON: No thanks. I'm hanging out with Alejandro. His mom made tacos. Can I stay here until nine?

Donnie's heart sank. He was happy his son had good friends to spend time with, but he wished Sebastian still liked being around him. It stung.

"You were right. He has better things to do than share a plate of wings with his old man."

"I'm sorry. He'll come around. Look at me, my dad totally sucked for most of my life, and we actually get along now."

"Yeah, it's just…" His throat was tight. "Hard sometimes, and I don't have anyone to lean on."

Ethan reached over and patted his friend's hand. Then he sat back in his chair. "Now that wing night is off the table. You can go to the concert. There's this app."

Donnie squinted at his friend. "An app?"

"Jax used it. Check your phone. Jax said they just sent you an invite code."

Donnie swiped his phone open and pulled his glasses down off his head so he could see. "Concert Buddies. What's that about?"

"Check this out. You set up an account that includes photo ID verification and you answer a survey. Then you can buy single tickets to the show if the person selling reviews your profile and accepts your purchase request. Once your purchase is approved, the app sends you the ticket and you can message with the person who sold you the ticket and meet up with them at the show. It's sort of like a safe way to have a blind date, but instead of love, you're looking for a concert buddy."

"It doesn't sound completely horrible. But I don't know."

"How about you think about it while you download the app and set up your profile?" Ethan asked.

"I suppose it can't hurt." Donnie stroked his beard as he considered. "I don't know if it's the small burst of caffeine I just had or if I'm actually warming to this idea."

"Dude, you love Eliza Fitzsimmons. Take a chance! What do you have to lose?"

"Stop giving me those puppy dog eyes. They might work on Mable, but not me."

Ethan tilted his head and frowned. "Are you sure about that?"

Donnie shook his head. "You are too handsome for your own good. I'm glad you don't use your powers for evil."

Ethan checked his watch. "I've got eleven minutes before I have to catch the train. Let's get this show on the road."

Donnie pulled out his wallet and took out his driver's license as well as a credit card. He snapped a picture and uploaded via the app. Then he handed Ethan his phone.

"Here, I need a profile picture for the app. Take a good picture of me."

Ethan shook his head. "Why am I not surprised you don't have a picture of yourself already saved on your phone?"

"I hate pictures of myself. I look like the Pillsbury Doughboy."

Ethan's brown eyes lit up with laughter, and he snorted. "More like you're one flannel shy of being a lumberjack."

Donnie smoothed his mustache. His cheeks went pink. "You're so full of it. Let's get this picture over with before I change my mind about the whole thing. Should I stand?"

"No, just cross your arms and I'll take the picture. Ready? Smile."

Donnie tried to remember if it was better to keep his chin up or tilted down. It was hard to think about anything other than how much he disliked having his picture taken.

Ethan took a bunch of pictures in quick succession and then handed the phone to Donnie to pick one. Donnie waved him off. "You pick. I'm not good at that sort of thing."

"You should think about why you're so harsh with yourself. Not that we have time to unpack that today."

Ethan scrolled through the options and chose a profile picture. He handed Donnie back his phone. "All done. Now find a ticket and make a friend. I've got to catch my train." Ethan hopped up, put on his crossbody computer bag, and rushed out.

Donnie yelled after him, "Thanks for the help!"

Ethan shouted back, "Can't wait to hear how it goes!"

Donnie closed the door and locked it. He still had time for his afternoon nap, but after talking to Ethan, he was too keyed up to lie down. He finished entering all his information into the app and then he left to head home.

***

Even though he was too long for it, his preferred relaxing spot was lying on his well-worn brown couch. He stuffed a throw pillow under his head and opened Concert Buddies. There were only three offerings for Eliza Fitzsimmons. He clicked on the first one, but it was for the standing room section of the venue. Donnie didn't think he'd be able to work tomorrow if he stood at a concert. He clicked on the second offer; the seat was in the twenty-fifth row. The requested price was in his range.

He opened the seller profile and saw the smiling face of a Black man wearing a Chicago Bears shirt. His name was Chris, he loved the Bears and Eliza Fitzsimmons, and he owned a bookstore on Chicago's South Side. Donnie quickly hit request to purchase. If he could go to the concert with someone who was not only a fellow Bears fan but also a bookseller, he was sure he'd have fun. Maybe he'd even make a new friend.

The app promised a response to all requests within thirty minutes, so Donnie decided to go take a shower and figure out what he'd wear to the concert if he did in fact go. As soon as he was out of the shower, he wrapped a towel around his waist and walked into his bedroom to check his phone. He opened the notification from Concert Buddies and read the note, "Sorry man, a friend off the app could go at the last minute, so I'm giving them the ticket. Best of luck. Go Bears!"

Donnie sat down on his bed, holding his phone. He should just forget about the concert. He could go see her another time, he tried to convince himself. Maybe it was because Sebastian had stopped wanting to spend time with him, or maybe it was because he knew Ethan was rooting for him to do something fun for a change, but he decided to give Concert Buddies one more chance. If that last offer was gone, then at least he could say he did his best to make it happen.

He searched the app again and saw that a new offer had just popped up. Donnie clicked on it and saw a woman's professional headshot. Her name was Susan. Her brown hair was up in a bun, and he wondered what it looked like when she wore it down.

The profile said that she had one tenth row ticket, and she was only asking for face value. He scrolled down on her profile and saw that her favorite song by Eliza Fitzsimmons was "How Can You Be Gone?"

He smiled and sent a request. This time, he added a comment with it.

"Hi! You're my last chance to see Eliza Fitzsimmons. I've been a fan of hers since 'Decorate Me' came out." He paused. What else could he say that might sway her if she had multiple offers. He started to make a pun using one of her song titles, "Please Wait No Longer," but when he read it back, he cringed. It sounded so cheesy.

In the end, he went with the truth. "I own a bakery that is also a bookstore, and I'm on my feet all day working. Getting to see Eliza would be worth the sleep I'll be missing out on." He double-checked his message for mistakes and sent it.

"Now what?" he asked aloud. "No sense sitting in a towel." He got off the bed and got dressed in a soft white T-shirt and a pair of brown corduroy pants. If he got the ticket, he could throw on a button-down shirt over the T-shirt.

Then he went into his bathroom. He ran a brush through his gray hair. On his shelf were three bottles of beard oil, he decided to use one that smelled woodsy. It had sandalwood, cedarwood, and a touch of peppermint. He inhaled as he stroked oil into his beard, enjoying how the scent made him feel like he was out in nature.

That was another part of himself he'd been neglecting. He knew that going for walks in the Marley Creek Nature Preserve was restorative, and yet he hadn't been there in months. Heck, he couldn't remember the last time he'd gone for a walk around the neighborhood.

His phone vibrated on the counter. He looked down and saw the Concert Buddies logo on the screen. He put on his glasses and opened the notification.

"Your offer has been accepted! You have eight minutes to complete the transaction. Once completed, your ticket will be listed under your events. Have a great night with your new Concert Buddy!"

Donnie quickly completed the transaction using the card he'd put on file when he opened his account earlier. Confetti streamed down his screen and fanfare played. "You're going to the show! Click here!" He clicked and the mobile ticket for Eliza Fitzsimmons 2024 North American Tour popped up. Donnie fist pumped and did a little dance as he made his way to his closet. He pulled a long-sleeve dress shirt off its hanger. It was a lavender windowpane shirt, and he thought it made his eyes look nice.

The next train into the city was arriving in twenty-seven minutes. Donnie finished getting ready and then he walked out to his car. He could park behind Books and Breads and walk over to the train station.

He sent a quick text to his son.

> DONNIE: I'm going to the Eliza Fitzsimmons concert tonight. Make sure you are home by nine.

> SON: You're going to a concert? How do I know this is even my dad.

> DONNIE: Funny. Just make sure you're home by curfew.

> SON: (thumbs up emoji)

Donnie pocketed his phone. The train horn sounded as it entered the station. He climbed the steps and walked through the cars until he found a double seat that didn't already have an occupant. He folded himself into the seat and waited for the conductor to come around and check his mobile ticket.

It had been decades since he'd taken the train downtown daily to work at the Hilton on Michigan Avenue right after culinary school. The only thing that seemed to have changed since those days was the free Wi-Fi. That and the cost of a ticket was almost double, but it still beat having to drive into the city and find parking.

A recorded voice announced, "Next Stop, Union Station!"

Donnie put in his earbuds and turned on Eliza Fitzsimmons. He tapped his feet and looked out the window as the skyline came into view.

Chapter Three

♥

Susan

Susan walked toward Michigan Avenue. She hoped she'd done the right thing selling her ticket online through that app. The guy she'd sold it to—what was his name? Dan? Dave? She checked her phone. Donnie, that was it. She'd had a handful of requests for her ticket, and it had come down to his eyes. His brown eyes looked sad. At first glance, she knew he was someone who needed a night of music to recharge his batteries.

Had she made the right choice? She'd find out soon enough.

The music in her earbuds stopped and ringing took its place. Susan fished her phone out of her jeans and saw Zaina's face displayed.

"Hi, babe. Are you excited?"

"I am excited about the show and a little nervous about meeting the guy. I still wish you were here instead."

"I wish I could be there too!" Zaina said.

"How's the swelling?"

"Jasper says it's definitely gone down. He told me I should have ankles again in no time, but I think he's just trying to make me feel better."

"Aw, hon. It's going to be okay."

Zaina sniffed on the other end of the phone. "I'm just worried, you know?"

"I know, but it's going to be okay," Susan repeated.

"Enough about me. Tell me more about your date."

"He's not a date. This is strictly a platonic concert buddy situation."

"Yes, right, totally, but tell me about him, anyway."

"His name is Donnie. I think he's probably in his forties. His hair is almost all gray and he has a full beard."

"Huh, that sounds like Donnie, the owner of Books and Breads. Wouldn't it be funny if the person you sold the ticket to was actually someone from right here in Marley Creek?"

Susan stopped in her tracks. "Books and Breads? The bakery that also has a bookstore. It has to be him! Looks like I went online to sell my ticket to someone who lives within a mile of me," She resumed her walking and got into the line queued up at the entrance of the White City Auditorium.

"This is great news! Donnie is a sweetheart; you're going to have such a delightful time with him at the show. Not for nothing, but he's single too."

"How do you know he's single?" Susan asked.

"Girl, you've been away from Marley Creek for too long. You know how everyone knows everyone's business!"

"Good point. I'd forgotten that side effect of small-town living." Susan looked at the line in front of her.

"It's not really that bad, the everyone in everyone else's business thing. I only know Donnie is very single because Jasper is friends with Donnie."

"Okay, thanks for explaining that part. Still, this isn't a date." Susan took a few steps forward as the line was moving.

"I know, but now that I'm happily married, I can't help wanting to see all my friends find their happily-ever-afters, too."

Susan rolled her eyes. She was just trying to get through each day and get her mother back on her feet. The last thing she needed was romance. However, now was not the time to get into that with her. Zaina was having an incredibly tough time, and if playing fantasy football with her friends' love lives was helping her cope right now, then so be it.

"I better let you go; the line is about to start moving."

"Have a good time! Make sure you post some pictures!" Zaina said.

"I will, and you get some rest."

"Ugh, I'm not built for rest, but I'll try. Bye!"

"Talk to you later!"

Susan bounced from foot to foot as she waited in line. She should have been reassured that her concert buddy was someone who was a friend of a friend of a friend, but instead, it raised the stakes for her. What if he was a total jerk and wrecked the concert vibes, and then she'd have to avoid running into him in town? This whole idea might be a total disaster. She took a deep breath. If Donnie was a jerk, she'd just concentrate on the show. She was there to see and listen to Eliza Fitzsimmons, not make a new friend.

The line shuffled forward and soon it was time to empty her pockets and get wanded by security. She was glad the app had allowed her to transfer the ticket right to Donnie. The last time she'd been to an Eliza Fitzsimmons concert, she had a printed paper ticket. It was hard to believe it had been over fifteen years.

She glimpsed her reflection in the door of the venue and that
snapped her back to the present day. She wasn't the same girl
she'd been then.

The hum of the crowd surrounded her, boosting her
excitement and calming her nervousness. To her left and right
were merch stands. She glanced over at the tour shirts, and
down at her boobs. The shirts looked like they were made for
kindergarteners. Plus, after spending so much for seats with a
great view, did she want to spend money on a shirt that might
be too tight in the arms and was cropped. It was enough to be
here tonight with only herself to worry about.

Susan checked the time. The opening act would be coming
on stage soon, but she had enough time to get a drink. She
waited in another line and ordered a hard seltzer. Then it was
time to find her seat. Would Donnie be here already? She was so
glad her seat was on the aisle. If Donnie was annoying, at least
she wouldn't be trapped in the middle of the row for the whole
concert. Susan showed her phone to the usher, who checked
her ticket and allowed her onto the main floor. Her stomach
fluttered as the stage got closer and closer.

Susan bopped her head to the Jason Isbell And The 400
Unit song that was playing and found row ten. She was the first
person to arrive in her row, and she realized that she'd be getting
up and down many times as her fellow concertgoers arrived.
But she was so happy to be out of the house, she didn't care.
It sure beat getting up over and over because her mom needed
something.

Her shoulders slumped. Those kinds of thoughts were
unkind; her mom had no one else. It was Susan's duty to take
care of her mother, and it wasn't like she had a job right now,

anyway. She clenched her fists. It made her so angry to think about the university dismissing her whole department—and by email, no less!

"Erm," said a deep voice next to her.

Susan whipped her head to the side and looked up. Gray hair, well-manicured beard, and those eyes—deep brown and full of melancholy.

She stood up. Susan was five-ten and Donnie towered over her. He had to be about six-three.

"Hi!" she said. His lavender shirt really made his eyes stand out. "You must be Donnie."

He ducked his head. "That's me."

"Great to meet you. I'm Susan."

Donnie put his hands in his front pockets. "Thanks for accepting my offer."

"You're welcome!" Susan moved forward to exit the row so that Donnie could take his seat, and Donnie moved, trying to get out of her way at the same time. She took a step to get out of the way and he moved in the same direction, accidentally blocking her. He held up his hands. His hands were huge. An image of those hands on her ass hoisting her up flashed in her head. A flush of heat flooded her body. Where had that come from?

She stood in the aisle, and Donnie took his seat. As Susan watched him, she now regretted they weren't in the middle of the row, so he had to brush past her as he sat down. There was something about him that made her crave physical contact. She closed her eyes for a moment to collect herself.

This was just because she hadn't had sex with anyone for over a year. Plus, since she'd been taking care of her mom, she hadn't even had the time or energy to take care of herself. Susan hadn't even unpacked her vibrator yet. The batteries were probably dead by now. Yes, that was it: just some late-thirties horniness setting in.

Susan gave Donnie a sidelong glance. He was tapping his foot to the music while he was on his phone sending a text. She hoped he wouldn't be on his phone all night. It was so annoying to be stuck next to people on their phones at concerts, plays, and movies. She liked to take a picture or two at the start of the event and then put her phone away so she could be in the moment. Onstage, a few crew members were adjusting microphones and tuning guitars. It looked like the opening act would begin soon.

"I hadn't heard of the opening band, Black Coffee Only, until I got the reminder text for the concert tonight," Susan said.

Donnie put his phone away and turned awkwardly toward Susan. Susan felt bad for him; he was a big guy just stuffed into the ancient seats. The White City Auditorium was over a hundred years old, and Susan doubted the seats had been updated. It certainly wasn't a very comfortable fit for her size fourteen bottom, either.

"Sorry about that. I needed to text my son," Donnie said.

"No worries. How old is he?"

"He's fifteen and over at a friend's. I am hoping he took me seriously when I told him to be home by nine."

"Sophomore?" she asked.

Donnie's lips were a straight line, and he nodded.

"Still working his way through puberty," Susan said. "That can be rough."

"Tell me about it. He won't stop nagging me to let him sign up for Driver's Ed."

"Are you going to?"

Donnie rubbed his face and then smoothed his beard. "Honestly, it's a long story. I don't want to get into it right now."

Susan frowned. "I'm sorry. I overstepped."

"It's okay, don't worry about it. How about you? Do you have any children?"

Susan pushed a lock of brown hair behind her ear. "No kids, no husband, currently taking care of my mom and living back at home after being downsized from Illinois State." She took a drink of her hard seltzer.

"Ah." Donnie appeared to be searching for words.

Susan put down her drink and waved her hand. "You don't have to come up with something to say. Like you said, it's a long story, no need to get into it now."

Donnie's face relaxed. He was probably glad this was just a concert buddy connection and not a blind date.

"Well, that was awkward," she mumbled. "I'm sorry that sounded rude. Life has just been exhausting lately, and this is the first time I've gotten some time to myself in weeks."

"Believe me, I know how that is," Donnie said.

Susan's smartwatch lit up with a text from Zaina. "Do you mind if I check my phone?"

"Be my guest. It's not like the show has started yet."

Susan opened her texting app and responded to Zaina's demand to know how it was going and told her all was well, and Donnie seemed nice. Zaina texted back a kissy face emoji. Susan replied with an eye roll emoji and put her phone back in her pocket.

Zaina could be a real pain in the butt sometimes, but her text had given Susan a good idea for a change of subject. She turned toward Donnie. "So, it turns out we have friends in common."

Donnie's eyes widened. "Really?"

Susan nodded. "My childhood friend Zaina who owns New Age Stone and Witch Crafts. She's the one who was supposed to be here with me tonight. She told me about the app."

"Zaina! It's really a small world, isn't it? How is she doing? Is everything okay?"

"Her doctor put her on partial bed rest, so she had to back out of the concert this afternoon."

Donnie's brows furrowed. "She and Jasper must be so worried. If you think of it, let her know I'm thinking about her, and if she needs one of my peanut butter dark chocolate chunk brownies, she can send Jasper over anytime."

Susan laughed. "I'm sure she'll take you up on that."

"Good. I heard about the app from my friend Ethan. He talked me into giving it a try. You were actually my last hope. I contacted someone else, but the ticket wasn't available anymore and I was running out of time."

"It's so wild to me that I wound up selling the ticket to someone who not only lives in the same town as me, but who knows my bestie," Susan said.

"Just a coincidence, or fate?" He held her gaze, and her pulse sped up. She leaned closer to him just as the opening act walked onto the stage. She quickly stood up and Donnie followed.

Black Coffee Only was a four-woman band. The lead singer grabbed the microphone and said, "Hey, Chicago! Are you ready to rock?" And they launched into their first song. Susan began dancing in place and Donnie joined her.

"I didn't expect the opening band to be so different from Eliza Fitzsimmons!" Susan yelled.

Donnie leaned down to her. He smelled like the forest preserve Susan had been meaning to start going on walks to. "I should have brought earplugs!"

"You're not wrong!" she shouted back and continued to groove.

The venue still had plenty of empty seats, so Donnie and Susan had an unobstructed view of the stage. After a couple of fast songs, Black Coffee Only slowed it down. The guitar player got behind a keyboard. Donnie slowly sat back down, and Susan followed suit. Donnie rubbed his knee through his corduroys and winced.

"Let me guess," Susan said. "An old college football injury?"

"More like too many hours standing in the bakery while being old and needing to lose about fifty pounds. "

"You do not need to lose fifty pounds!"

Donnie rolled his eyes.

"Seriously," Susan insisted. "Women like men who are tall and broad-shouldered. And you're a baker; you're probably hoisting bushels of flour daily."

Donnie grinned and this time his smile reached his eyes. She wanted to reach up and trace the little crinkles around his eyes that were now sparkling. They looked like summer sunsets, and she wanted to sit and stare at them all night long.

"The flour I buy comes in fifty-pound paper sacks."

"Exactly what I was saying, sort of. You're lifting tons of weight daily. It's good that you are brawny."

"Brawny, like the paper towels?" Donnie asked.

"You even look like the guy on the package!"

They looked at each other and Susan quirked her eyebrow. Donnie began laughing, and Susan followed suit.

"I do tend to wear flannel shirts come November." He winked at her. "Do you want another drink? I'm going to go get a beer."

"Yes, thank you." She pulled a twenty-dollar bill out of her pocket and handed it to Donnie.

He put up his hand. "I got this."

"Are you sure?"

Donnie nodded and walked toward the lobby.

The band was playing another slow song and wrapping up their set, so Susan sat back down. As soon as she did, an usher was at her side directing four people into her row. She stood in the aisle until the two couples sat down. Before she bothered to sit back down again, she checked to see if Donnie was on his way back yet, and he wasn't, so she sat down and pulled out her phone to text Zaina.

SUSAN: Donnie is wonderful. He is kind, and honestly, he's pretty hot.

ZANIA: He's like a big cuddly teddy bear who also makes the best brownies ever!

SUSAN: Speaking of, he told me to tell you if you crave any, send Jasper right over.

ZANIA: Aww, see, aren't you glad I talked you into the app?

SUSAN: Yes. I am!

Susan looked up and saw that Donnie was walking back with a beverage in each hand.

SUSAN: Gotta go! Donnie is back.

She put her phone away. Donnie handed her a seltzer, and she moved into the aisle. He stood in front of his seat and waited until she was next to him.

He raised his beer, and she lifted her seltzer.

"Cheers," she said, and they tapped their cans.

"To new concert buddies?" he said.

She grinned widely, and they both took a drink.

"These are great seats! We're smack dab in the middle of the main stage," he said.

"I know, right?" She grabbed Donnie's forearm. "Look, they're bringing out Eliza's grand piano!"

Donnie put down his drink and squeezed Susan's hand. Her stomach fluttered. Was it because she was about to see her favorite artist on stage or because she was seeing her with Donnie?

Chapter Four

♥

Donnie

Susan's hand was in his! Their hands were entwined and Eliza Fitzsimmons was about to take the stage. This was by far the best night he'd had in years. Her hand was strong but small in his. He was afraid to look down at them and break the spell. He was trying to stay in the moment and not overthink how he was feeling right now. But she was holding his hand!

He had little experience with dating outside of Maggie, and that had been over twenty years ago. Sure, this wasn't supposed to be a date...but had they veered into the date zone? What would Sebastian think?

Donnie's hands were sweating now. He removed his hand from Susan's and rubbed it on his jeans. For years now, Donnie had been sure the best thing for him to do was to wait until his son went off to college before trying to date. But now, for the first time, he didn't want to keep waiting.

Susan turned to Donnie. "I'm going to run to the bathroom before the concert starts. I don't want to miss a second of her set!"

"Do you need me to watch anything for you?"

Susan shook her head. "I didn't bring a purse. Oh, but can you hold my drink?" She handed him her can. He took it and as he did, their hands brushed. A thrill went through him.

She stood and started walking up the aisle. The venue was nearly full now. He turned his head and watched her weave her way out to the lobby. She had a great-looking ass. He allowed himself to imagine her in his bed, bent over in front of him. Donnie bet she'd turn and look at him over her shoulder, egging him on.

He felt she might have as much pent-up desire and need for connection as he did. When she looked at him, he recognized the want in her eyes, and it wasn't for sex. She looked like she was completely maxed out and if she didn't do something to let off some steam, she might break down. Or maybe he was projecting.

Donnie took a long pull of his beer. He didn't drink often, and this was a high alcohol IPA. Maybe the beer was hitting him, or it was the buzz of excitement around him, because he could not remember the last time he'd found himself ogling someone. If anyone had told him yesterday that he'd not only be at a concert, but actually taking the step of holding a beautiful woman's hand, he wouldn't have believed it. Donnie hoped this wasn't a dream.

Two people were now pointing toward the two empty seats on the other side of him. He moved out into the aisle, holding his beer and Susan's drink, and let the couple in. They were wearing matching Eliza Fitzsimmons T-shirts emblazoned with an image of her sitting behind her piano.

"Love the shirts," he said as they walked by and took their seats. He looked for Susan, but didn't see her in the wave of people that were continuing to walk down the aisles for the start of the show. On the stage, crew members were still checking instruments and adjusting lighting and microphones. Donnie bounced his leg, hoping Susan would be able to make it back before the concert started. He enjoyed being with someone who loved Eliza's music as much as he did. She got it. Now that he was here, he was glad Sebastian hadn't come with him to the concert. Sebastian would have come begrudgingly, and he would have been on his phone the whole time.

Donnie had forgotten how nice it could be to spend time with someone who listened to what you said and had similar interests. Again, he thought maybe it hadn't been such a good idea to put off dating for so many years.

Finally, Susan approached and slid into her seat. Donnie's pulse quickened.

"You would not believe the line for the bathroom!" She turned toward him and put her hand on his forearm again. He wished he'd worn a short-sleeve shirt.

"I'm glad you made it back. I was afraid you'd miss her coming on stage."

Susan squeezed his arm. "I'm so excited! What song do you think she'll play first?"

Donnie took a drink of his beer and thought for a moment. "Are we making a bet?"

Susan paused. "Should we? What would we bet?"

Donnie grinned. "That's an excellent question." Susan licked her lips, and Donnie followed her pink tongue with his eyes. He wanted to say, *let's bet a kiss*. Instead, he said, "You tell me."

Susan broke eye contact with him and looked at the stage. She pushed her wavy brown hair behind her ear. Then she turned and snapped her fingers. "If I win, I want brownies."

Donnie put out his hand. "If you win, I'll make you your own brownie flight."

Susan shook his hand. Was she slow to let go of his hand, or was he imagining things? "You have brownie flights?"

"No." He paused. "I should, though, don't you think?"

"God, yes, the world needs brownie flights. Now tell me what song Eliza is going to play first."

"I think she'd going to start with one of the songs off her new release, so I'm going to guess 'Right On Time.'"

Susan's eyes sparkled. "I love that song—one of my favorites on this album. It helps me when I'm feeling depressed about living back home without a job, taking my mom from doctor appointment to doctor appointment."

Donnie squeezed Susan's hand. "I'm sorry about your job."

"Thank you. I appreciate that. But like the song says, maybe my life is right on time and now is when I'm in the season of taking care of family."

"I hear that," Donnie said. He wondered what kind of job Susan was looking for and if he knew anyone who was hiring. He opened his mouth to ask more about her career and job needs when the lights went up and the crowd got on their feet.

Susan jumped out of her seat. She clapped her hands above her head and her shirt rode up, giving Donnie a glimpse of her midriff. The crowd began to chant, and he pushed himself out of his chair and joined Susan on her feet. He realized they never said what she would give him if he won the bet, and frankly, he didn't care. He felt like he'd already won the night.

"Eliza, Eliza, Eliza!"

The tiny brunette with waist-length hair waved to the crowd as she took her place behind the piano. The crowd chanted and then Eliza started playing the first chords of "Right on Time."

Susan stood on her tiptoes, leaned into him, yelling into his ear. "You were right, you won the bet, and we didn't even talk about what you got if you won the bet!"

He wrapped his arm around her waist. "Being here with you and Eliza, I feel like I've already won the lottery."

***

Two and a half hours later, Eliza left the stage, and the crowd of elated fans slowly exited the auditorium. Donnie's knees were aching, but he didn't even care.

"Did you drive tonight?" Susan asked.

"I took the train. You?"

"I drove."

"Can I walk you to your car?"

"I'd really like that, and you're in luck. My car is on the way to the train station. What time is your train?"

Donnie stopped and pulled out his phone and his glasses. "My train isn't until eleven. I'm sure I can walk you to your car and make my train." Susan stood by his side. She was moving from side to side. "You okay?" he asked.

Susan rubbed her bare arms. "I debated wearing a coat, but it was warm enough to go without one earlier."

Donnie put his arm around Susan. "Let's get you to your car." The walk sign lit up and they crossed the street.

"What a concert, huh?"

"It was better than I could have imagined." He gave her shoulder a squeeze. "Thanks to you accepting my offer. Eliza played all the songs I was hoping she'd play, plus I got to meet you."

"And I got to meet you. The only downside was you guessed the first song, so I don't get to have a brownie flight."

"You have an open invitation to come to Books and Breads for brownies any day of the week. Well, except Monday. We're closed on Monday."

Susan pointed to the parking garage in front of them. "I'm here."

"I'll come up with you, just to be safe," Donnie said.

"I'm sure I'll be fine, but yes, come with me."

They entered the parking garage and stood waiting for the elevator.

"What are you going to name the brownie flight? Something fun?" Susan asked.

"'Brownie flight' isn't fun enough? It's definitely self-explanatory."

"Do any of your items have fun names?" Susan's eyes were sparkling again.

Butterflies fluttered in his chest; she liked him enough to tease him. Maybe he should ask her out on a date. "My menu is user friendly. The bacon, egg and cheese on sourdough, for example."

"What's the fun in that?"

The elevator doors open and they walked out. In the vestibule, the Chicago Bears fight song was playing.

"Ah, we're on the Bears floor. That's easy to remember. Are you a fan?" Donnie asked.

"Only as much as anyone who grew up around here. You?"

"I didn't grow up around here, so I'm a fan by choice," Donnie said.

"Adopted our team, huh?"

"They had a couple good years when I came to Illinois for college, and I like orange and blue. What can I say?"

Susan clicked her key fob, and a car horn beeped and lights flashed. "That's me!" She picked up her pace, walking away from Donnie. "I should have bought a car with a remote start, and heated seats."

Donnie chuckled and caught up to her in a few strides of his long legs.

Susan opened her car door, hopped in, and started her car. Then she got back out and leaned against her door. He put his hand on the top of the door frame. Susan looked up and he was lost in her deep brown eyes.

"Thanks again for making sure I got to my car safely; it was very kind of you."

Donnie raised his other hand, wanting to caress her cheek. He stopped himself, unsure if he should. "I'm glad I got to spend a little more time with you."

She bit her lip and then smiled widely. "What a show, huh?"

Her bottom lip was like a plump berry, and he wished he could lean over and taste her.

"Tonight is a night I'll never forget," he said. Her long eyelashes framed her big brown eyes. Warmth pooled low in his abdomen. He wanted to pull her to him, wrap his arms around her, and bury his head in her neck, kissing her pulse point. He needed to know what she smelled like.

As if she could read his mind, she placed her hand on his shoulder and gave him a kiss on his cheek. She smelled like orange blossoms and vanilla, and it made him think of delicate cookies that would melt on his tongue. "I don't want you to miss your train."

Instinctively, Donnie pulled his phone out of his pocket and checked the time. "Shoot, you're right. I've got to get going."

"I'll take you up on the free brownie soon."

"You better." He tried unsuccessfully to hide a grin when he saw her reddened cheeks. She was cute when she blushed.

"I'd pinky-swear I'll be in this week, but with taking care of my mom, I can't make any promises. I'll try, though."

"I'll take it. See you soon, Susan."

Chapter Five

♥

Susan

Susan woke up later than usual. She'd forgotten to set her alarm clock, but the rising sun had awoken her before eight a.m. The mattress on her childhood bed was a far cry from the one she had in storage, so she gave up trying to go back to sleep. She would have been fine if she'd gone to sleep right after she'd gotten home, but she'd been too keyed up. Instead of taking a melatonin gummy, she'd stayed up half the night watching videos and reading posts on social media about the show.

She'd also taken the time to follow the public page of Books and Breads. She searched Donnie's name as well. He didn't have much of a social media presence outside of his bakery/bookstore. That could have been because he didn't have much use for it, or it could have been that Donnie was a smart businessman focused on his brand. Having spent time with Donnie, she was pretty sure it was both. So many small businesses didn't survive their first few years, and he'd managed to find success in a small town with two very different businesses under one roof.

She did find a news story from about ten years ago describing a young mom who lost her life in a terrible car accident in Marley Creek. A truck driver had fallen asleep and run a red light just as Maggie Larson was driving through the intersection. Susan's heart sank. Poor Donnie, poor Donnie's son—what was his name? Sebastian. How awful for them both.

"Suzy? Are you up? I need help."

Susan tossed her phone on her bed and walked downstairs to her mother. If only she could have a minute to make herself a cup of coffee before having to tend to her mom. She walked into the living room. Once Dorothy had been released from the hospital after the surgery to help repair her broken hip, Medicare had covered delivery and set up a hospital bed on the main floor of the house.

The plaid couch dating from Susan's youth was pushed against the wall. Susan had taken the coffee table out to the garage and stored it next to her mom's dust-covered sedan. The bed was in the middle of the space, facing an entertainment center with a TV. Susan had found a rolling table to put by it, so at least her mom could easily eat or drink. Next to the entertainment center was the so far unused walker and by the bed was the rented wheelchair.

Susan was nearly used to how small her mom looked in the bed and the transformation of the living room, where she had played video games back in the day, into a recovery room. "I'm here." she said.

"I need a nicotine lozenge. The lady last night moved some stuff around and now it's not with my other medication."

Susan walked over to the side table, which was covered with medications, a couple of glasses, and a clean ashtray her mother had refused to let her put away. She moved the medicine bottles around, looking for the package of lozenges. "Mom, your doctor said you really shouldn't have any of these while you are healing."

Dorothy worried the edge of her sweater. "I'm only taking three a day. It's that or I swear to God I'll figure out how to use the Uber Eats app and get a carton of cigarettes delivered. Do you want that to happen?"

"Of course, I don't want you to start smoking again. Look what smoking did." Susan waved her hand toward the bed and the wheelchair.

"I know; we both read the pamphlet from that nurse about smoking and osteoporosis."

Dorothy put out her hand in a gimme motion. Susan dropped the package into her mother's hand. Her mother struggled to push a lozenge out of the blister packaging. "These damn hands. My right hand is worse than ever since they stuck those IVs in me." She tried again to open the package. "Damnit," she said gruffly. "What are you waiting for? Help me out here!"

Grinding her teeth, Susan took the pack. "Hold out your hand."

Her mother did. Susan popped the lozenge out and into her mother's palm. She noticed how her mother didn't try to close her fist around the medicine. Instead, she put her whole hand up to her mouth.

"Does your hand hurt? Here, let me see it," she said.

Susan reached for her mom's hand, but Dorothy pulled her hand back. "It hurts when I wake up. It'll be fine in a little while."

Susan backed away. "Fine, I'm going to make some coffee. Do you need anything else from me?"

"Help me get in the wheelchair. I need to use the bathroom."

Susan helped transfer her mom from the bed to the chair, then pushed her mom down the hall to the powder room. It was a real balancing act because the wheelchair didn't fit through the door.

Dorothy sucked on the nicotine and didn't speak as Susan helped her get situated. It was an unspoken rule that neither Dorothy nor Susan spoke unless absolutely necessary when Susan helped Dorothy use the bathroom or shower. Susan understood her mother had always done everything by herself, and her new limitations had taken most of her dignity and the miniscule amount of good humor Dorothy had left. Her mom had always been overbearing and miserable, but at least she used to laugh once in a while. For years she'd gone to the community center once a week to play cards. Now Dorothy was stuck, unable to do almost anything by herself, and it wasn't like anyone was coming over to hang out with her.

Susan transferred her mom back to the chair and handed her mom a wet wipe.

Dorothy wiped her hands off and handed the wipe back to Susan, who threw it away. "You know, I'd really prefer to wash my hands."

The lack of caffeine was causing a headache to brew—or was it her mother? "Sorry, but it's not my fault the wheelchair doesn't fit through the door."

"You don't need to yell at me," Dorothy said.

"How am I yelling? I'm just using my regular voice."

"You know what I mean."

"I—you know what? Nevermind." Susan took a deep breath and pushed her mom back into the living room.

"Take me to the kitchen. I'd like some coffee." Just hearing about coffee relaxed Susan. She pushed her mom into the kitchen and made them a pot.

***

Susan unloaded the dishwasher after lunch while her mother napped. She put in her headphones and started listening to her top twenty most-played songs. Eliza Fitzsimmons was thirteen of the top twenty.

As the song began, Susan was transported back to last night with Donnie. She wished she could drop everything and run over to claim her brownie—hopefully, he'd make her a flight—but that wasn't possible. Either she'd need to take her mom with her, or she'd need to find respite care for a couple of hours. If her mom hadn't been such a pill, she wouldn't have minded taking her along, but as it was, she would not put herself or Donnie through that.

Seeing Donnie again would have to wait until she could arrange care. After the dishes were finished, Susan opened her laptop and pulled up her emails. In her inbox was an email marked urgent from Helping Hearts, the only elder care organization in Marley Creek that took Medicare and offered a sliding scale for additional fees. Her heart stopped. Her mom was so cantankerous it was hard to find even temporary respite workers who would come back after their first experience with her mother. She clicked on the email only to find her worst fears realized; Helping Hearts would no longer provide respite care unless Susan was at home as well.

"Not much of a respite if I can't leave the premises," Susan mumbled. She scrolled the email to see if it included any information about what happened last night. The only thing she found was a sentence that read:

"Caregiver stated the client made her uncomfortable and she would not return to the home."

Susan yelled into a hand towel she'd left on the table. Since she'd arrived last month, she could not get her feet under her. Between mourning over the loss of the job she'd had for over a decade to providing care and support to her mother in spite of their long-strained relationship, Susan felt like she was walking through quicksand. She would have to get to the bottom of what had happened last night and see if there was any way Helping Hearts would reconsider. It was that, or she'd need to dip into her savings to pay for care, just so she could get out for a few hours once in a while.

Susan looked up at the calendar on the wall. Just a little over three weeks until her mom's next appointment with the surgeon. If all was healing well, Dorothy could move on to physical therapy and increasing the use of the walker. If things weren't going well, there could be another surgery ahead. Susan really hoped no more surgeries were needed. She'd like to get back to her own life.

Susan scoffed at her thoughts. She'd lost her job, her work friends were scattered all over now that their department had dissolved. She didn't even have her condo to go back to. The only anchor she had right now was her mom. This was not where she had expected to be in her late thirties. Even the comforter on her bed hadn't changed.

The next email was an invitation to her twentieth high school reunion. Marley Creek High School always had their reunions the weekend before Thanksgiving, and that was only a little over a month away. Susan leaned back in her chair and deleted the email. No way was she going to go to that. Her phone rang. She checked the display to see which of her mom's medical providers was calling and was pleasantly surprised to see it was Zaina.

"Hey, what's up?"

"I want to hear all about last night. Then we need to talk about the reunion." Zaina said.

"I'm not going to the reunion."

"But you have to! It will be a blast."

"A blast? What's with the nineteen-sixties slang? Going to high school wasn't a blast, and I am certain the reunion won't be either."

"Come on, we had fun! Remember when we went on the choir trip sophomore year? That was super fun!"

"Z, remember I didn't go on the trip? My mom refused to sign the permission slip, even though I had saved enough money to go."

"Ugh, I'm so sorry, I totally forgot about that! That really sucked for you," Zaina said.

"Thanks."

"But you should still go! We had lots of fun in choir, remember?"

Susan smiled, remembering how she had enjoyed being part of it, even though it had meant being at school by seven a.m. for practices. "We did have fun. Remember the pep rally when I fell off the riser?"

"I can't believe you didn't break your ankle! We were terrible. I laughed so hard I had a cramp in my side the whole day," Zaina said.

"I laughed the hardest, and I was the one who fell. I'm glad you talked me into joining freshman year. It was one of the few extracurricular activities that my mom would allow me to participate in because she thought choir was all girls and I wouldn't be around any boys."

"Geez, I forgot about that too. Your mom was such a buzzkill! You didn't get to have hardly any fun," Zaina said.

Susan sighed. "She's not much better now, but these days, I can ignore her opinions."

"She's lucky to have you. I hope she realizes that! If not, I'll get out of this bed and come set her straight."

"You're the best. But I'm still not going to the reunion."

"Okay, got it. We'll put a pin in it for now and talk about it later."

Susan didn't say anything.

"Tell me about the concert! And Donnie—especially that part!"

"Eliza was amazing! Her voice was as good, if not better, live than it is on her albums. She played everything I wanted to hear, plus she sang almost everything on the new release. It was amazing! I don't know how she does it. It was such a great time."

"I'm so bummed I missed it. I watched clips the tour posted. You are so lucky she played 'Sunshine Fades Everything Good'! I love that song."

"I always forget that's your favorite Eliza song. It's so sad. It doesn't match your personality, if you ask me. You're a ray of sunlight. I'm surprised you like it," Susan said.

"It's the way she's able to make you feel her longing for her love to never end, even though it's clear the relationship is already over. She gets me every time! And to hear it live! I might have fainted."

"All the more reason it was good that you weren't there. We can't have you fainting," Susan said.

"I didn't really mean it literally. I hope this tour goes so well that Eliza doesn't wait such a long time to tour again."

"For sure."

"Did you have a nice time with Donnie?"

Susan's cheeks heated as she remembered the way Donnie looked at her when they'd almost kissed. "We had a fantastic time. It was a night to remember."

Zaina giggled. "I don't think I've ever heard you talk this way. Even when you got engaged to what's-his-name."

Susan laughed. "You can use his name. It's been about seven years since the divorce."

"I still don't like the way Ray treated you."

"Thanks for holding my grudges longer than me. You are a true friend."

"I'm always on your side. Now give me more scoop on you and Donnie. I lost the remote, and it's the only way to control our smart TV. I need entertainment."

"There isn't too much to tell. Eliza was amazing. Donnie is as big a fan as we are, so I'm super glad he got the ticket, since you couldn't go," Susan said.

"And?"

"His eyes are such a rich shade of brown, but are so sad, almost all the time. He's like a big burly lumberjack, but it gets even better, because he bakes and reads books." Susan chuckled. "I called him brawny, and he said, 'like the paper towels?' and I said, 'exactly.'"

"You are smitten, and it sounds like he is, too! Did he ask you out? Did you ask him out? What's the scoop?"

"He was a total gentleman. He walked me to my car. I-I—"

"Did you two kiss?" Zaina interrupted.

Susan sighed. "I think we almost did. You know that feeling when it's like you're magnets, and you know he's looking at your lips? And you are being pulled closer, like you just want to melt against him?"

"That's how Jasper makes me feel even now when I'm as big as a house." Zaina sighed, "I think he's into you."

"I did kiss his cheek when we said goodbye. I thanked him for everything and gave him a peck," Susan confirmed.

"I'm going to call this a date of convenience. This was your first date of many with Donnie."

"Nice of you to say, but I don't know if he sees it that way."

"Are you going to see him again?" Zaina asked.

"No set plan, but he invited me to Books and Breads to try his brownies."

"Did you just say brownies, or did my pregnancy hormones cause me to mishear?"

"No, that's what I said. Donnie invited me to stop by Books and Breads anytime and he'll give me a sampling of his craft brownies. I called it a brownie flight."

"He should totally start selling that. I'd send Jasper over the second it was available. Everything he bakes is amazing."

"Right? I think he is going to add it to the menu," Susan said. "When are you going to go?"

"That's the thing. Either I take Mom along, and you know how she can be, or I have to find respite care, and that's getting tougher and tougher."

"What about Helping Hearts?" Zaina asked.

"That's who I've been using, but right before you called, I got an email saying based on another complaint last night from now on, they won't provide care unless I'm home, too."

"That really defeats the purpose, doesn't it?" Zaina said.

"It sure does. I'm going to talk to my mom and get to the bottom of what happened last night, and maybe I'll be able to get Helping Hearts to give us another chance."

"I'll keep my fingers crossed. You're still going to the fall festival Sunday, though?"

"For sure. I was planning to bring Mom to that. I'm hoping maybe being around other people will cheer her up a little," Susan said.

"I'll see you there. I have to sit and skip all the fun activities, but I've got to support my man."

"He's lucky to have you."

"You're exactly right! I'll talk to you soon. Text me if you have your brownie date," Zaina said.

"It's not a date," Susan said

"That's what you said about the concert, and it was!"

"Bu—"

"Bye!" Zaina ended the call.

Susan shook her head. She was glad Zaina was in her corner. Too bad Zaina couldn't be there for backup when Susan confronted her mother about the caregiver issues later tonight.

Chapter Six

❤

Donnie

The door swung open and Donnie's heart leapt. Maybe this time it would be Susan. A steady flow of customers had been coming in all day and each time, no matter how he tried to tamp it down, his heart raced as soon as he heard the door. He turned and saw it was a woman with a little boy.

Donnie checked his watch as they walked over to the table where board books for children were displayed. Sebastian should be here by now to work his after-school shift. It wasn't like him to be late. Donnie's stomach roiled. He pulled out his phone and called his son.

Ring, Ring, Ring, "Sup, this is Bastian's phone. Don't bother leaving a voicemail. I won't listen to it."

Donnie whispered, "Dammit." He ended the call and fished his glasses out of his pants pocket. He opened his texts. No texts from Sebastian.

His heart was pounding in his chest. He understood he was overreacting, but even after years of therapy, he still had a very hard time when anyone didn't show up when they were supposed to. He'd lived the worst-case scenario when Maggie had been late coming home. That day he'd been so angry with her and had assumed she decided to go out after work just to get back at him for the fight they'd had.

"Excuse me." The young mother was holding a copy of *The Very Hungry Caterpillar*. "Is this part of the buy one, get one half off sale?"

"Yes, ma'am, it is. All the books on that table are part of the BOGO."

His hands were sweating. He looked down at his phone, nothing from his son.

The mother spoke again. "I'm ready to check out."

Donnie dropped his phone into his pocket. "I can ring you up here." The woman and her child walked up to the counter and Donnie scanned their purchases. "Would you like a cookie for your kiddo?"

The woman bit her lip.

"They're free." He pointed. "The little sugar cookies here. I make them extra small and frosting-free for little hands."

The woman smiled in relief. "Oh, that's so nice of you." She turned to the boy who Donnie guessed was around three years old, "Do you want a cookie?" The small boy wearing overalls and sporting a little afro nodded his head.

Donnie used tongs and put two of the small cookies in a cellophane bag and handed it to his mother. Then he bagged up her books and added a flyer with the list of upcoming story hours to the bag. She took the bag. "Thanks for coming in," Donnie said.

"Thank you for the little treat! We'll be back."

They left the store. Donnie whipped his phone back out. Still no word from Sebastian. He texted him again and used some fire alarm emojis to get his point across. Then he went into the kitchen to work out some of his stress by stretching and folding his sourdough. If his son didn't get to Books and Breads by the time he was done prepping today's batches of bread, he was going to call the police. Well, maybe that was overkill. He'd call the school first.

He pulled and stretched the dough until he got it all out. Then he took off his gloves and checked his phone. No new texts. He called the school.

Ring.

The door wooshed open. Donnie looked up and relief flooded every cell of his body.

Sebastian walked into the bakery, mumbled, "Hi," and stowed his backpack under the counter.

"W-Where have you been?" Donnie tried and failed to keep his voice down.

"Bruh, why are you screaming at me? What if a customer walked in?"

Donnie clenched his fists. "Son, where have you been? I was worried," he said, his voice back to normal range.

"Band practice, Dad. Same as usual."

Shoot, he was right. Donnie had totally forgotten. "I'm sorry. You know how I worry. I'll try to remember to check the calendar before I start assuming something happened to you."

"Whatever," Sebastian said and he looked back down at his phone, his fingers flying over the keys.

Donnie rolled his eyes, but his heart was happy. His kid was here where he could see him, and all was well.

Donnie went back into the kitchen to wrap up preparations for the next morning. Once he was done, he walked back to the front of the bakery to talk to Sebastian. "I'm heading out. I have lasagna ready to put in the oven. When you get home, we can throw together a salad and have that for dinner."

"Fine," Sebastian said, not taking his eyes off his phone.

"See you later."

Sebastian looked up. His thick brown hair was in his eyes, and he brushed it back with his free hand. "Cool, I've got a paper for you to sign from school."

"You're not in trouble, are you? Did you get a bad grade?"

"No, it's not that. I need parent permission for driver's ed. We start driving after winter break."

Donnie's stomach dropped into his shoes. This was a nightmare. A flush of heat rushed through him.

"Erm, I've got to run. We'll talk later."

Donnie rushed out the door to his car. He stopped and leaned on the SUV. As he'd ran, his throat started to close. His vision was starting to tunnel. He threw himself into the driver's seat and started the car. Hot air blasted out of the air vents and he prayed the air conditioning would kick in and help short circuit the heat overwhelming him.

He closed his eyes and focused on his breathing. It had been years since he'd had a full-blown panic attack. It was clear to him that Sebastian being late, had primed his nervous system. If not for that, maybe his son simply mentioning being behind the wheel wouldn't have upset him so thoroughly. Twenty minutes later, Donnie had calmed down enough to feel safe to drive home.

***

Lasagna still bubbling from the oven was one of Donnie's favorite fall and winter meals. But tonight, it was tasteless mush in his mouth. He pushed the food around his plate while Sebastian wolfed down his food, still giving all his attention to his phone.

Donnie couldn't prolong this any longer. It hurt his heart to disappoint his son, but he needed to keep him safe.

"Do you have that paper from school?"

"I'll go get it right now." Sebastian hopped up and ran out of the kitchen to his bedroom. Moments later, he was back. He put the paper down in front of his father. "All you have to do is sign this permission slip and put down your insurance information, and I'll get to drive on the road."

Donnie put on his glasses and read the form. If it weren't his child and if he didn't know exactly how car accidents destroyed families, he'd have no problem signing this piece of paper. Even though the page was short and easy to understand, he re-read it before he was ready to respond to Sebastian.

"I'm not going to sign this paper right now."

Sebastian looked up from his phone, squinting as if trying to see his father better. "What do you mean? Do you need to wait until the end of the month? I don't think you have to send a check for any fees."

"It's not that."

"Do you need your insurance card? I can run out to the car and get it." Sebastian pushed back his chair and got up.

"Sit down, Son. It's not that." Donnie stroked his beard.

"What's wrong? I'm on the honor roll, I don't drink, you let me get my permit through the school—why can't I start driving? It's not fair!"

Inwardly, Donnie groaned. He knew he should have made Sebastian wait until next school year to get his permit. Then he wouldn't be having this conversation. But Sebastian had begged and begged, and last June, this moment had seemed far off. Donnie fidgeted with his paper napkin, crushing it into a ball and then flattening it out on the table.

"Dad, are you even listening to me? God! You're the worst!"

"You need to spend more time paying attention to what's going on around you. Whenever I see you, you have your head in your phone, especially when we are in the car. You need to be watching how I'm driving and the flow of traffic. You need to learn by watching first. Then next summer we can revisit you being behind the wheel."

Sebastian's face, the mirror of his mother's, was bright red. "No effing way! I hate you!" he screamed. He stomped out of the kitchen and up the stairs to his bedroom.

Donnie slowly got up from the table. He had to grip his plate, which was still full of lasagna with two hands; he was shaking so much. At least his son hadn't run out of the house. Maybe once Sebastian had a chance to sleep on it, he'd understand the importance of being ready to drive. Cars were deadly weapons.

Donnie's stomach was still unsettled, so he made a cup of tea and put on Eliza Fitzsimmons's new album. On vinyl, it was almost as good hearing her live. As the first song reached its chorus, Donnie's thoughts were filled with Susan. The way her eyes had sparkled, her voice cracking when she was singing along with the crowd for the encore, and how her lips had felt when they'd brushed against his cheek.

Why, oh why, hadn't he asked for her phone number? Now he only had three potential ways to contact her, and a couple of them were plain embarrassing. He could send a message through the app and hope she saw it. He could ask Ethan to ask Jasper to call him, and then he could ask Jasper if he could get Susan's number from Zaina. Or he could just wait and hope she came into his shop.

Doing nothing seemed like the best way to go. He rubbed his chest. Now that he'd settled on no course of action, he thought he'd feel better. Instead, he walked around feeling like his shirt was a size too small.

Chapter Seven

♥

Susan

Susan needed to find out what the heck had happened with her mom and the caregiver on Friday so she could fix it. Hoping a full stomach would make her mom more receptive to talking, she planned to wait until after dinner. Then she decided she'd better clean the kitchen. She loaded the dishwasher, wiped the counters, and swept the floor. She might have skipped sweeping the floor, but last week Dorothy's wheelchair had run over some crumbs, and her mom had complained that they were one step away from a rat infestation.

Finally, the kitchen was spotless. Susan walked out to where her mom was in bed watching television.

"Mom, you got a minute?"

Dorothy paused the TV. "I was in the middle of this show. What do you need?"

Susan sat down in the wingback chair. "Can you tell me what happened with the Helping Hearts lady when I was at the concert? Were there any problems or issues?"

Dorothy narrowed her eyes. "Everything was fine, aside from the fact that she was pretty lazy. It probably wasn't her fault. I think she wasn't all there. I told her to make me a cup of coffee and she gave me tea instead. And she kept trying to talk to me. Kept asking me if I wanted to use the bathroom. You know I hate that. I'm not a child and I won't be treated like one. She should've left me alone and just done what I asked her to do. Is it that hard to find good workers?"

"Mom, did you yell at the lady? Did you say anything else?"

"Do I ever yell?"

Susan shook her head. Her mom had never been a yeller, she just wielded passive-aggressive comments like a weapon.

"Can I get back to my show now?"

"Yeah, fine, go ahead."

Her mother resumed watching a medical drama. Susan sat and thought about what her mother had said. She must be leaving something out.

"You didn't tell the lady she was lazy, did you?"

"No. I should have, but I didn't."

Susan propped her feet up on the ottoman. Had her mom done anything to upset the worker? Sure, she was abrupt and often rude, but the employees at Helping Hearts had to be used to cantankerous elderly clients. Susan decided to watch the hospital show with her mom instead of scrolling on her phone. She would call Helping Hearts tomorrow and see what could be done. An ad came on the television for a weight reduction medicine.

"Suzy, have you looked into that medicine?"

Susan spoke through clenched teeth. "I have not."

"You should. Look, it says it can help you lose at least ten percent of your body weight in the first six weeks. That's probably at least twenty pounds for you, right? Your class reunion is coming up. Don't you want to be closer to your high school weight for that?"

Susan bit her knuckle. She had never understood why her mom judged people based on their weight. The woman made no comments about anyone's race, sexual preferences, or country of origin, but she was always commenting on people's weight.

Susan was glad she wasn't the same size she'd been in high school. Back then, she'd internalized her mother's fatphobia and had constantly deprived herself of what she wanted to eat, in order to stay at a weight that left her hungry more often than not. It had taken years and lots of therapy to get to a place where she appreciated all her body could do and allowed herself to enjoy food. She liked her curves. She loved the clothes she'd found that accented her thick thighs. Thank goodness she lived in a time when the culture at large appreciated a woman who had an ass to match her D-cups and her heart-shaped face. She was strong and soft. Her mom was weak and wiry. Susan didn't want to wind up in her mother's shoes one day, unable to see people for who they were, not what size they wore.

A lightbulb went off over her head.

"Mom?"

"Yes, dear?"

"What did the worker who was here look like?"

"She was a big girl. Bigger than you, but a little taller. I told her about that medication, too. She would be pretty if she lost some weight. That's why I told her not to help herself to any food she saw in the kitchen. Especially the donuts on the counter."

Susan put her hands over her face. "Are you freaking kidding me? No wonder she doesn't want to come back here. Why can't you stop obsessing over people's sizes?"

Dorothy plucked at her blanket, agitated. "I was trying to be helpful; I was thinking about that girl's health."

"It's not helpful, Mom. It's rude. And now what are we going to do?" Susan threw up her hands in frustration. "The agency won't send anybody else to come out here because of your behavior unless I'm here, too! We were already on our last chance after the time you yelled at the lady to go buy you cigarettes! You can't yell at people who come here to help you, or no one is going to help us." Susan glared at her mother, only to see Dorothy practically smirking.

"It's probably for the best." Dorothy crossed her arms. "They don't get very good people to work there. I heard the pay stinks, and they probably think we're just all charity cases. They don't really care about me. Let's face it; at this point, I'm worthless to society. They'd be happier if I was in a coma then they could sit and read their books or be on their phones the whole time they were here. You'd be happier too, I'm sure."

Susan rolled her eyes. "Of course I wouldn't be happier. They're just trying to do their jobs. Why do you have to be so mean?"

"Why do I need to be nice?" Dorothy retorted. "If they did their jobs, I would be perfectly pleasant, but they don't do anything but sit and look at their phones, and I don't like it. What would be so bad about playing cards or working on a puzzle with me?"

Susan looked at her mother and noticed the sallowness of her skin and the bruises that still marked her hand from the IV.

White hair had grown out, leaving her previously dyed blonde hair looking dull and yellow. Susan's heart ached, knowing her mom was so lonely.

Maybe if she took her mom for a cut and color, she'd get to spend some time around people outside the house. Hopefully, her mom could behave in public, and Susan could help her get a boost of confidence with a fresh hairstyle and companionship. Then again, her mom was acting like a stray dog. Desperate to be petted, but when you tried to pet him, he snapped at you and tried to bite your hand. Susan added finding a hair stylist for Mom to her list of tasks for the week. That to-do was as important as the medical appointments they had coming up.

And while they were out, perhaps they'd stop at Books and Breads so Susan could take Donnie up on his offer of a brownie flight. If she had to wait until she figured out new respite care, it could be weeks before she'd be able to get over and see that brawny man. If she had to take her mother with her, then she would.

Chapter Eight

♥

Donnie

It was now day three of Sebastian giving Donnie the silent treatment. Donnie hated it, but he hated the idea of Sebastian being behind the wheel more.

It had almost been a week since the concert and he'd yet to see Susan. He was starting to give up hope. Maybe he'd misread the situation at the concert and Susan wasn't interested in him. That was probably for the best. This way he could stick to his plan not to date until Sebastian was off to college, which was only a couple of years away.

Besides, he had a business to run. It was the fourth quarter, and that was when he made the profits that helped him make it through the rest of the winter. Just keeping Books and Breads going and working on events like the fall festival would keep him busy enough to forget about Susan.

Donnie continued reviewing the inventory of his cooler. He needed to run by Hop's Heaven and pick up some of Jasper's Oktoberfest beer to use in his Bavarian Pretzel recipe. Last year, they'd gone through over fifteen hundred pretzels during the fall festival. Donnie had offered to provide them at cost for the event again this year, but just like last year, Jasper had insisted on paying a discounted price that was well above cost. Donnie smiled; he was lucky to live where the small business owners took care of each other. He didn't know what he'd do if he didn't have this place.

The timer buzzed, and Donnie walked over to the oven. His afternoon batches of bagels were ready to take out and cool. As he finished placing the bagels on wire racks, the front door chimed. He left the kitchen and walked out to greet his customer. His pulse quickened when he realized who it was pushing an older woman in a wheelchair into his shop. It was her! His heart took flight, and he rushed over to help her navigate the store.

"Susan! It's so nice to see you. I was afraid you'd changed your mind—" His face flushed, "about the free brownie, I mean."

"Sorry it took me so long," she said.

"No worries—it's only been a few days." The energy zinging around his body because he was talking to her belied the casual tone of his voice.

Susan's mother cleared her throat loudly.

"Sorry, Mom. Donnie, this is my mother, Dorothy. Mom, this is Donnie, the owner of Books and Breads. We met at the concert last week."

Susan's mom was slight, the wheelchair dwarfing her. She wore a gray sweatshirt with the word 'fall' in applique on the front. Her hair was in a blonde bob. Her small brown eyes squinted up at him.

"We were over at Shannon's Shears getting Mom's hair done. Since we were close by, I thought we should stop."

Donnie took off his glove and held out his hand. "It's a pleasure to meet you, Ms. Brown." Dorothy clasped his hand. Donnie noticed she had faded bruises on her hand and shook her hand gently.

"Well, you are certainly a big guy," Dorothy said.

Donnie felt his ears turn bright red. He looked up at Susan, who had her hand on her forehead.

"Mom."

"I didn't mean anything by it. He's a big guy." Dorothy turned to direct her question to Donnie "How tall are you?"

"I'm six-three."

"See, he's a big guy. You need to calm down, Suzy. You told me to be on my best behavior. I'm on my best behavior." Dorothy folded her hands in her lap.

Donnie glanced at Susan. Her cheeks were red, and she was biting her lip. Donnie willed himself not to hug her. Instead, he put on his customer service hat. "Would you ladies like to try a pumpkin spice latte or a cup of chai?"

"I'll take a cup of black coffee. Decaf, if you have it," Dorothy said.

"Coming right up."

"I'll try a chai," Susan said.

"Suzy, I want to sit by the windows. It's chilly in here."

"Do you want your lap blanket?" Susan pulled the tote bag emblazoned with the Illinois State logo and began rummaging through it.

Dorothy waved her off and Susan wheeled her mother to the table. Donnie focused on making a decaf pour-over for Dorothy and a chai latte for Susan. Since it was nearly two-thirty, most of his baked goods were gone. Over the years he'd perfected his pour-over technique, so he dared to look at Susan while he poured water over the grounds.

She was wearing a lightweight fuchsia sweater with a deep V-neck. He was willing to bet that the creamy skin of her decolletage would taste as good as the vanilla cream he made to frost his cinnamon rolls. His cock hardened and he was grateful that he was wearing an apron over his work pants. He finished the beverages while thinking about cleaning the bathroom. Once the thought of toilet bowl cleaner had cooled his ardor, he walked over to Susan and her mother. He placed the drinks in front of each of them.

"Dorothy, do you need any cream or sugar?"

Dorothy frowned. "I said I wanted black coffee, remember? This is decaf, I hope."

"Yes, ma'am, it's decaf. I'm sorry about that, my mistake." Donnie was glad he'd been in the service industry for so long that any rudeness from customers rolled off his back. He remembered that Susan had said her mother suffered a fall, so he'd chalk up her tone to any pain she might be feeling. Susan looked up at him and mouthed *thank you.*

"Don't think I forgot I owe you some brownies," Donnie told her. "Unfortunately, we are running low on baked goods right now. Would you like our last double chocolate chunk brownie?"

"Yes, let's do that." She smiled widely and again Donnie had the urge to wrap his arms around her. He smiled back, happy that she seemed more relaxed now.

Donnie went to the bakery case and took out the large brownie. He put it on a plate with a knife and carried an extra plate and two forks over to the table. He placed everything in front of Susan.

"Donnie, are you busy? Or can you sit down and chat for a few minutes?" Susan asked.

Warmth spread in Donnie's chest. "I'll pull up a chair." He moved a chair over to their table and sat down.

Dorothy took a sip of her coffee. "It's better than I thought it would be."

Susan held up her hand next to her mouth. "That's her version of high praise."

Donnie laughed. "I'm glad you are enjoying it. You'll have to see how you like it with the brownie."

"Chocolate's fattening. I'm not going to eat that."

Donnie fell silent. His bakery was usually a haven where people came seeking chocolate goodness. Dorothy was a real hard nut to crack.

Susan pulled the brownie to herself. She cut an eighth of it off, put it on a plate, and pushed it across the table to her mother. Then she took a bite of the rest of the brownie. Donnie watched her brown eyes light up in delight. "Oh my goodness, this is heavenly. Mom, you've got to try it. The chocolate chunks are dark chocolate, and the brownie is surprisingly fluffy."

Her tongue darted out. Donnie's mouth watered as he watched Susan lick her fork clean. What would it be like for her to lick him like she licked the chocolate off? He bit the inside of his mouth to stop from groaning.

"Mom, just have a little sliver, so you can give it a taste."

"Now you're making me look rude to your friend." Dorothy said. She held her coffee cup in her hand, and Donnie was glad that he'd ordered lightweight coffee cups for in-store customers. They were non-breakable as well.

"No worries." He gave Susan a wink. "The best time to get my brownies is before noon. Or you can call and let me know when you'll be in, and I'll put some aside for you—we can try out your brownie flight idea."

Susan's mouth was full of brownie. Donnie's heart swelled; he liked watching her eat his cooking. She did a little shimmy as she chewed. She had no shame in showing her enjoyment. A thrill went through him as he watched her eat. Maybe he should just go for it and ask her out. It clearly hadn't been easy for her to trek over with her mom, but she'd made the effort. Now all he had to do was find the nerve to ask for a date.

"Would you like to—" he started to say when Sebastian walked in the front door.

"Hi, Son," Donnie said. Sebastian walked by. He had his earbuds in, but Donnie was sure he'd heard him. His bangs were in his face, and he ignored them as he walked to the bookstore section. It was Sebastian's afternoon to work while Donnie did paperwork and went home early.

"So that's your son," Susan said.

"Yep, that's Sebastian. He's not happy with me right now."

"Is everything okay?" Susan asked.

"It's fine."

"Are you a single dad?" Dorothy interjected.

"What makes you ask that?" Donnie said.

"I remember having that look on my face when she was in high school." Dorothy gestured with her thumb at Susan. "I don't think she was happy with me much because I was the only parent, and I was the only one to say all the 'no, you can't do that's.'"

Donnie frowned. "You might be on to something there; I'm a single parent, and I did have to say no."

Susan pushed away her empty plate and sipped on her chai. Donnie was defeated. The mood had shifted, and he couldn't ask Susan out now. He should have just done it that night at the concert, and now he'd blown his second opportunity.

Dorothy put down her coffee cup and shifted in her wheelchair.

"Mom, are you okay?" Susan asked. She leaned toward her.

Her mom frowned. "I'm ready to go. My pills are at home."

Susan stood up and checked her smartwatch. "Shoot, it's already after four, we've got to go." She put her tote on her shoulder and began cleaning the table.

"You can leave that right there," Donnie said. "I'll take care of it."

Susan pulled out a small lap blanket and put it across her mom's lap. Then she looked up and made eye contact with Donnie. "Thank you so much. It was so nice to see you again."

"Let me walk you two out." Donnie walked over to the front door and pushed the automatic door button. The door swung open. "Are you planning to go to the fall festival on Sunday?" he asked. Butterflies swirled as he waited for her response.

"Yes, Mom and I are planning to go around lunchtime. Early afternoons work best."

"Fantastic. I'll see you there."

Susan gave him a smile. "See you soon."

Chapter Nine

♥

Susan

Caring for her mother was exhausting, both mentally and physically. What got Susan through most days was knowing the situation was temporary. It would take time, but her mom would be able to go back to taking care of herself, and Susan would be free to go back to her life.

Her stomach clenched. Could she go back to her life? That was questionable, at best. First and foremost, she needed a new job. It made her sick to think about the way the university had dismissed her after years of bosses promising her she was on track to become a department head.

Twenty years past high school, and she was starting over from scratch. At least she had the net proceeds from selling her condo. Unless she wound up paying thousands of dollars out of pocket for caregivers because her mom didn't know how to act around people. Susan wondered if there was a group or a club for older people to make friends in Marley Creek. Was she wrong in thinking her mom wasn't as mean when she was growing up? She remembered her mom had even hosted Tupperware parties and craft nights from time to time. What had happened to those ladies? Susan sighed; she sure hoped they all hadn't passed away.

Susan rolled out of bed. That was enough life reflection for a weekend morning. Today was the town's fall festival, and Susan was going to see Donnie. The thought of spending time with him put a smile on her face, and even knowing she would have Dorothy in tow didn't bother her. Susan put her feet in the slippers at her bedside and headed downstairs to see if her mom was up and needed help in the bathroom.

Susan peeked into the living room and was happy to see her mother was still snoozing. *Bonus, I might get to have a relaxing cup of coffee!* She tiptoed into the kitchen and brewed a pot. Taking out the biggest mug she could find, she added a nice base of pumpkin spice creamer and filled the mug to the brim. Being able to have a moment to collect her thoughts before caring for her mother was a rare treat. She sat down at the kitchen table and pulled out her phone to text Zaina.

> SUSAN: How's it going?

> ZAINA: Jasper said he's going to lock me in the house if I try to go to the festival.

Susan's blood pressure rose. She knew Zaina was exaggerating, but when men made high-handed decisions about the women in their lives, it ticked her off.

> SUSAN: Sounds like he's nervous about you and the baby. Will I see you this afternoon?

ZAINA: He is a worrywart, I'll be there. My blood pressure is in the normal range and I don't have a headache or anything.

SUSAN: Great! Tell Jasper I'll sit with you and make sure you aren't running around.

ZAINA: I can't wait to see you and Donnie together. Make sure you come inside the brewery with him so I can say hi. (heart eyes emoji)

SUSAN: (thumbs up emoji)

Susan could hear her mother stirring in the next room. She knew her mom would try to get in her wheelchair and take herself to the bathroom. "Mom, do you need help?"

"I'd like to do this myself, if you don't mind."

Susan stood next to the bed. She positioned the wheelchair so that her mom could transfer herself into it. Her mom started to move, and Susan held up her hand. "Let me make sure the wheels are locked. One sec." Susan confirmed it was locked. She nervously watched her mother maneuver herself.

When Dorothy was situated, Susan unlocked the wheelchair and followed her mother to the bathroom. Her mother had only started attempting to use the bathroom on her own the day before, and she wanted to hover to make sure she was there to stop any potential fall. If her mom had a setback, Susan didn't know if either of them could handle it, but she understood how proud her mom was.

Sweat beaded on her back. It seemed like it was taking her mom forever. "Is everything okay?"

"Yes, dear. Please leave me alone."

Susan wanted to say, *I'd love to, old woman, but you're all I've got.* Instead, she said nothing and remained ready in case of emergency.

"Did you make some coffee?" Her mother asked as she rolled down the hall. Susan nodded, and they went into the kitchen for breakfast.

***

That afternoon Susan was grateful she'd remembered to put her mom's handicap placard in her car. Otherwise, she would have had to push the wheelchair three blocks just to get to Hop's Heaven for the festival. The forecast had hinted at rain, which would have been a disaster, but there wasn't a cloud in the sky and she didn't even need a jacket. Susan had been so focused on wearing something cute since she was going to see Donnie that she hadn't thought about how much of a sweat she worked up every time she had to push her mom around.

"I don't know about you," she huffed, "but I'm going to be happy when you graduate out of this wheelchair."

"Think of it this way. I'm helping you get a much-needed workout." Dorothy said.

"I'd rather you walk on your own and I go to the gym for a workout."

Susan waited for another biting remark from her mom. But she didn't say anything. In fact, unless her eyes were deceiving her, her mom had nodded. Susan would take the win. They entered the festival area.

Susan looked around to see if she recognized anyone. "Mom, do you see anyone you know?"

"I doubt anyone I know would be here; besides, I don't get out much." Her mom folded her hands in her lap.

"How about a glass of cider?"

"That's a lot of sugar."

Susan gritted her teeth. "It's the fall festival. Treat yourself."

Under a blue and white checkered tent, a band played "Brown Eyed Girl" to a small crowd. To Susan's left was the children's area which included games and a table of small pumpkins where kids and their parents sat decorating. On the right was a railcar that had been converted to a food stand. The smell of brats and grilled onions made her stomach growl.

"Do you want to get in line with me? Or do you want me to find a place for us to sit and eat, and you can stay there while I get our food?"

"I'll stay with you; I don't like sitting by myself." Dorothy frowned and mumbled, "I look like a sad sack already, stuck in this wheelchair."

"Okee-dokee," Susan said.

Because the festival was free including the food, the long line moved quickly. When they got closer, Susan's heart jumped. Behind the counter, in a neon orange volunteer shirt was Donnie. She waited impatiently for their turn. Someone in the audience listening to the band yelled "Freebird," and the band ignored that request and instead began to play "September" by Earth, Wind, and Fire.

"Do you want a hot dog or a brat?" a woman with wavy brown hair in a ponytail asked her mother.

Susan did a double take. "Nicole Garrett, is that you?"

"Susan!" Nicole smiled and gestured a hugging motion with her hands. "Zaina told me you were back in Marley Creek! How are you? We have to get together!"

"I'm good. Congratulations on your marriage!"

Nicole blushed. "Thank you! Sean is here, too. He's the chef behind all the food today—well, except for Donnie's pretzels." Nicole pointed with her tongs at Donnie, who had his back turned helping a young couple.

"Where is Sean? I'd love to meet him."

"He had to run some food into the brewery for Jasper's staff." Susan nodded.

"So, what can I get you ladies?" Nicole asked.

"I'll take a hot dog, I guess. I don't think I've had one in decades, but it's less fatty than a brat, so give me that," Dorothy said.

Nicole leaned down and handed Dorothy an aluminum-wrapped hot dog. "Did you want any chips?"

"No thank you," Dorothy said.

"How about you, fellow MCHS Mustang?"

"Don't remind me, I can't believe our twentieth class reunion is coming up! I'll take a brat with lots of onions," Susan said.

"Coming right up!" Nicole handed Susan a brat. "Are you going to the reunion?"

Susan shook her head, "I don't know."

"You have to go!" Nicole looked behind Susan and saw people waiting patiently in line. "I wish we had more time to catch up."

"Me too," Susan said.

"I tell you what, Zaina, Devin, and I have a girls' night coming up. Can I have Zaina text you the info?"

"That would be great!" Susan said excitedly.

"Cool! See you later!" Nicole said.

Susan and Dorothy moved down to where Donnie was giving out pretzels.

Donnie's eyes lit up as soon as he saw Susan. She smiled in return.

"You made it!" he said.

"We were hoping to get here a little earlier, but it took a little longer than we expected to get out of the house," Susan said.

Dorothy chimed in. "Susan couldn't decide what to wear."

"Y-you look amazing."

Susan's face flushed. "Thank you."

"I'm due for a break. Give me ten minutes to find someone to take my place serving. I could come sit with you ladies—if that's all right?" Donnie said.

"Will you be bringing us pretzels?" Dorothy asked.

Donnie and Susan looked at her in surprise.

"Of course!" Donnie said. "Did you want one with salt or with cinnamon sugar?"

"I'm not one for sweets. Better give us the regular one, easy on the salt." Dorothy said.

Susan loved cinnamon sugar, but she wasn't going to push it. If her mom was going to treat herself for once, Susan wouldn't get in the way. "See you soon," she said.

Susan found a table on the outskirts of the band tent. It was far enough away from the band that they'd be able to hear each other talk. Susan made sure her mother was comfortable and then she sat down to eat. Even though she'd arrived at the fest hungry, the anticipation of spending time with Donnie sitting close enough to touch had her so distracted she barely touched her food.

"How's your food, Mom?"

"It's pretty good." Her mom had already finished half of her hot dog. Maybe it was the lack of fresh air and other people that had pulled her mom into such a funk. Susan mentally crossed her fingers. Could she get that lucky? Did her mom just need company?

"Here comes your big friend. I figure the pretzel must be good. He must eat a lot, right?"

Susan felt a headache coming on. One step forward, two steps back.

Donnie pulled up a chair and sat next to Susan. She realized he was close enough that if she turned toward him, their legs would touch. So, she did just that. He placed a small box in front of Dorothy and opened it. Inside was the tortilla-sized Bavarian pretzel with two small containers. "I didn't know if you'd like to dip your pretzel, so I brought you brown mustard and the Hop's Heaven beer cheese."

Dorothy looked at the pretzel and the dips. "Which do you prefer?" She broke off a small piece of the pretzel.

"I like both. It just depends if you are a mustard person or not."

Susan looked at her mother. "Try the mustard. You're clearly a mustard person."

Dorothy pursed her lips. "How so?"

"You don't even keep ketchup in your house."

"Too much sugar," she said and made a face.

"The beer cheese is also very savory," Donnie said.

Dorothy opened the mustard and dunked her pretzel piece in it. She chewed her small piece and then pushed the box over to Susan.

Susan froze, embarrassed. Why had she come here with her mother? She was about to insult Donnie.

"You don't want any more?" Susan managed to get out and immediately regretted asking.

"Donnie, that was a nice pretzel—crunchy on the outside and fluffy in the middle. The mustard was a good choice. That's for letting me try it."

Donnie grinned. "I'm glad you liked it. Plenty more where that came from."

"We will have to come back to your bakery soon. Maybe I'll look at the books too," Dorothy said.

Susan's stomach unclenched. She pulled off a piece of the pretzel and opened the beer cheese. She popped the piece in her mouth and chewed. It was delicious.

"That pretzel is amazing, Donnie!"

"Thanks." Donnie put his hand on her leg. She felt warmth low in her belly. Once again, for a totally different reason, she questioned coming to the event with her mother.

Dorothy's shrewd eyes narrowed, and she turned away from Donnie and Susan toward the stage. "This band isn't terrible."

Susan bit her lip. She really wanted to have some time alone talking with Donnie. "How much time do you have before you need to go back to serving food?"

Donnie pulled out his phone and checked the time. "I told Jax I'd be back by two, so about twenty minutes?"

"I told Zaina I'd come visit her in the brewery. Do you want to come with?"

"I'd love to."

"Mom, do you mind if Donnie and I go into the brewery to see Zaina?"

"That's fine, I'll stay here. You kids go ahead."

Susan stood up and gave her mom a kiss on the cheek. Then she turned to Donnie. He held out his hand, and she took it.

Chapter Ten

♥

Donnie

Several of his toes had gone numb a few hours ago, and his knee was killing him. He'd only managed to catch a few hours of sleep, and he'd been so excited to see Susan he'd forgotten to eat. None of that mattered now, because she was holding his hand. This time he wasn't going to waste his chance.

"Would you go on a date with me?" he blurted out before he lost his nerve. His heart pounded in his ears in the seconds that followed. Had he made a mistake? Why would this stunning, intelligent woman go out with him? A big schlub of a guy who had at least one bad knee and spent all his time keeping his small business afloat. What did he have to offer?

"I would," she said.

He squeezed her hand in his excitement. "Are you free Saturday afternoon? I close Books and Breads at three. We could go over to Jessie's Pub? Football will be on."

"Sure! That sounds like fun."

Donnie started walking faster, his former knee pain no longer an issue. "I'll pick you up at four."

Susan stopped walking. Donnie almost tripped; he was so focused on heading into the brewery. "What's up?" His stomach felt uneasy. Had he made a mistake?

"Give me your phone. I'll put my info in it."

Donnie's brow relaxed. He was an idiot, and he needed to stop jumping to conclusions. He unlocked his phone and handed it to Susan. She quickly typed in her information and handed it back to him. Just as he was about to put it back in his pocket, she grabbed his hand.

"Wait! Let's take a selfie, and you can use that for my avatar."

"I love it," he said before he even realized he'd just offered to be in a picture. What was going on? He hated having his picture taken.

Susan held his phone and stood on tiptoes. He leaned down a little. She framed their faces and took a burst of pictures. He smiled widely. Her smell was so enticing he couldn't stop himself from kissing the crown of her head. She shivered, leaned back against his chest, and showed him the pictures.

"Which one do you want to use?"

"Whatever one you like best."

"But it's your phone. You're the one who's going to have to look at it all the time."

"I'm not good with this stuff, really you decide. I trust that you'll know which one is the best." Donnie said.

"Okay." Susan swiped through and picked one. She saved it to her contact and showed it to him. "I like this one the best. You look so cute in it; I just want to reach out and give you a hug."

Donnie put his arms around her and squeezed. Her ass was pressed against his jeans, and he knew she could feel how attracted he was to her. He had to use all his self-control not to rock against her. "You look beautiful in all the pictures, full stop. But in this one, you look like you are having so much fun. Whenever I see your contact on my phone, I'll smile."

She turned and touched his cheek. "That was so sweet."

He bit the inside of his cheek; he wanted to kiss her right here in the middle of the fall festival. Their date couldn't come fast enough. She took his hand and led him into the brewery. He wondered how happy he would be if she led him around for the rest of his life. The shock of that thought startled him so much that he tripped over his own feet.

Susan stopped and turned to him. "Are you okay?"

He regained his footing and smiled, then whispered into her ear. "I think I got so distracted by your ass in those jeans, I almost fell."

"Head over heels?" She quirked an eyebrow. Then she turned to wave at Zaina, who was sitting at a table near the back of the brewery.

Donnie followed Susan as they wound around the back to Zaina. She was in an office chair with her feet up.

"Look at you, living the life of luxury!" Susan exclaimed.

"I would be if Jasper didn't check on me approximately every three minutes. Please sit down and keep me company for a little while. Maybe then he'll leave me alone and focus on his work."

Susan said, "Sure thing." She and Donnie pulled out chairs.

"Donnie, you're a man," Zaina started to say.

"Uh-oh. I don't like the sound of that," Donnie said.

Zaina put a finger up. "Hear me out."

"Go on."

"Jasper is causing me more stress than he is saving by hovering over me."

Susan and Donnie nodded. Susan patted Zaina's hand.

Donnie sighed. "Think of it this way, he's probably terrified he might lose both of you. So he'll do whatever it takes, up to and including wrapping you in bubble wrap."

Zaina sighed. "I guess I see your point. Any chance you can have a talk with him?"

Donnie nodded, "I can give it a try."

"Maybe he'll listen to you. I don't think he's hearing what I'm saying, but enough about my problems. How are you two? Is this a date?" Zaina smiled like the Cheshire Cat.

Donnie's heart sped up. What was Susan going to say?

Susan pulled her thick hair to the side. Her exposed neck called to Donnie. He wished this was a date. But since he hadn't gone on a date in years, he considered this afternoon much-needed practice before they had their first date later that week.

"No, we are not on a date. I'm here with Mom, and Donnie is on a break from the long hours he's spending helping to make today a success."

Zaina's hands moved over her belly.

"Is the baby kicking up a storm?" he asked, remembering the days when Maggie was pregnant with Sebastian.

"She is." Zaina beamed.

Donnie knew he had a goofy grin on his face, but he couldn't help it. He could feel Susan looking at him. He hoped she didn't get the impression that he wanted a new wife whom he could have more kids with. It hadn't been so long since he stopped wearing his wedding ring and he'd never envisioned himself having more children. He was a single dad with one son, and that had always been good enough for him.

"We left Mom back at the tent listening to music, but we should probably head back," Susan said.

"Yes, totally. You can't leave Dorothy out there by herself. Unless you think that could help her get out of her depression. Maybe she's making some new friends out there?"

Susan shook her head ruefully. "I wish, but I don't see any scenario where she strikes up a conversation and makes a friend."

"We're going to have to figure out what to do with her. She needs a community," Zaina said.

Susan rolled her head on her shoulders. "Tell me about it. I have to live with her."

"Speaking of friends—Nicole said she invited you to our girls' night at my house."

Donnie chuckled and Zaina gestured at him. "See, you get it. Everyone has decided to take over for me. Nicole is inviting people over to my house and Jasper is walking behind me like I'm a toddler learning to walk."

"I'm sure it's not that bad."

"Let me be annoyed."

"Oh, for sure, and yes, Nicole did invite me."

Zaina clapped her hands. "You can come, right?"

Susan paused for a moment; she bit her bottom lip. Donnie wondered if this was a tell. Was she about to lie?

"Yes, I'll find someone to watch Mom, and I'll be over."

"Maybe you can bring me some brownies as well?"

Susan and Zaina looked at Donnie.

"Your wish is my command. Just let me know when you want to pick them up," Donnie said.

"Fantastic. I need some of your yummy brownies in my life." Susan stood up. "We better get back to Mom."

"Enjoy the rest of your pre-date," Zaina teased.

Susan rolled her eyes and took Donnie's hand. They walked out of the bustling brewery and went around the back of the building, taking a shortcut back to where Susan's mother was waiting.

Donnie's phone alarm went off. "Crap, I better go back to the rail car." The shortcut was free of other people.

"Can I get a hug before you go?" Susan asked.

Donnie pulled Susan into his arms. She encircled his waist with her arms and buried her head in his chest. He kissed the top of her head again, but it wasn't enough. He tilted her head up and caressed her cheek.

"Susan Brown, may I kiss you?"

"I would love that."

Donnie froze for a second as he realized Susan was the first woman he was kissing since Maggie. He closed his eyes and pressed his lips against Susan's full lips.

She was intoxicating. He melded himself into her. Wanting to deepen the kiss but understanding she needed to get back to her mother, and he needed to get back to serving the people of Marley Creek, he sighed and broke it off. Donnie swallowed a smile when he noticed she was also trying to catch her breath. She pushed her hair away from her face, and he was mesmerized by her rosebud lips. He wanted more of her.

"That was..." she began.

"Amazing?" he finished.

"I was going to say delicious."

"That also works for me." Donnie pulled their clasped hands toward him and kissed her hand. They arrived back at the music tent far too quickly for Donnie. He let go of Susan's hand.

"This was really fun," he said. "Thanks for making time to come out today."

"I was afraid the afternoon was going to be a disaster. It's hard to take my mom out places, but now I wish we could stay longer," Susan said.

"Me too," he said, looking into her eyes.

"We'll have to save it for our date."

Donnie gave a half smile, "Sounds like a plan."

Chapter Eleven

♥

Susan

Susan's phone died mid-phone dial. She put it on the charger and then walked over to the landline she was now grateful her mother had never gotten rid of. Susan pulled back her hair, twisted it up, and secured it with a pencil. She looked down at her notebook, fourteen different elder care groups in the area were crossed through. No one had respite care available for a new client.

Susan listened to the nightly news theme play in the living room. She'd been on the phone for hours. Now it was down to the last number on her list. Susan punched in the eight-hundred number and then pressed one for English, and then listened to her options, none of which applied to the reason for her call.

"Operator," she finally said, and the automated system hung up on her. She shook the receiver; it was that or slam the phone down. She hit redial. This time she waited to be routed to the receptionist. Since Monday she'd been working on finding someone to watch her mother so she could go to girls' night out. Now it was only a few hours away and she still didn't have respite care.

"Thank you for calling H.O.P.E. You've reached the after-hours voicemail. If this is an emergency, please dial nine-one-one. Otherwise, leave a message and someone will get back to you during the next business day."

Susan disconnected the call and closed her eyes. Today was not going as planned, and she really needed some girl time. It had been a long week; her mom was more snappish than usual. Susan had taken her temperature and looked for other signs of infection. Thank goodness it wasn't that. Maybe her mom's temper and general crabbiness were simply due to being unable to get up and walk around like she'd been used to doing her whole life.

Susan tried to put herself in her mother's shoes. She'd be angry too. Susan made a mental note to work on researching what she could do to help her mother not feel helpless. But for now, the best thing she could do for both of them was find someone who was willing to hang out with her mom for a few hours so she could relax and maybe even laugh. And most importantly, she had to find someone to cover for her when she went on her date with Donnie. The last thing she wanted to do was to cancel that date.

Her phone buzzed, and a text from Zaina popped up on the screen.

> ZAINA: Donnie has a box of brownies for me. Any chance you can pick them up before you come over here?

Susan looked at her phone. Should she tell Zaina yes, even though she didn't have anyone to watch her mom? Susan took a deep breath in and stretched. She walked around the kitchen and listened to the sportscaster talk about college football in the other room. She was supposed to be at Zaina's in less than two hours. Should she give up and stay home? Or ask Zaina if it was okay for Dorothy to come with?

The laptop on the kitchen counter pinged. Susan looked at the screen and she had a private message from her post on the Marley Creek community page. One of the group members Susan had messaged with before was a Certified Nursing Assistant and she was able to watch Dorothy tonight.

Susan clapped her hands. This could work! She messaged Abigail and asked for her phone number.

Abigail messaged right back. Susan punched in the number and crossed her fingers that she was able to talk.

"Hi Abigail, It's Susan. Do you have time to talk?"

"I have a few minutes."

"Great, thank you so much for the message. I just need someone here with my mom for a few hours while I go to a friend's house. I'll only be a couple of miles away."

"How much care will your mom need?"

"She may need assistance getting to the bathroom and transferring to bed. There shouldn't be much work. She will need to take medicine, and she'd probably like for you to talk with her or play cards or Scrabble—something interactive if possible."

"Okay, that shouldn't be a problem at all. I work at Creek Rising Rehab. You can check online."

Susan pulled up the website for the rehab facility and looked up Abigail's online employee profile. She'd been there for over ten years.

"Everything looks good, and we've talked online and in person, so that helps as well," Susan said. "Plus, I know where you live!"

"That's right—you picked up zucchini off my porch last month."

"I used it to make zucchini bread. It turned out great," Susan said.

"You'll have to message me the recipe."

"Definitely. I'll send it with my address. I'd like to leave around six-thirty. Does that work for you?"

"That would be cutting it close, but I can make it by a quarter to seven?" Abigail said.

"Great, and I'll be home by ten. How much will it be?"

"Since it's such late notice and I've already been at work all day, I really need two hundred and fifty to be fair," Abigail said.

Susan covered her mouth to hide her gasp. She'd expected the cost to be half as much. Not working and taking care of her mom was emotionally and financially taxing. She would pay this time, but she needed a better long-term solution.

Susan gulped and answered. "Two-fifty works. I'll see you in a little over an hour."

Susan ran to the steps of Zaina and Jasper's house. Then she remembered her bag was filled with a dozen craft brownies Zaina had asked her to bring from Donnie's and she slowed down. This wasn't a formal event. There was no need to be stressed out because she was late. They would understand she'd had to make sure her mom was comfortable before leaving. She knocked on the door. She'd been so flustered today that she'd forgotten Zaina had a long-storied history of being late, so it really didn't matter.

The door swung open. "Susan's here!" Nicole shouted over her shoulder and then she hugged Susan. "It's so nice to see you again. I'm so glad you are joining us tonight." She gave Susan a squeeze and let her go.

"I thought I wasn't going to make it tonight."

"You'll have to tell us what happened during the venting portion of the evening. I made real and mock sangria for that. Give me your coat. I'm playing host while Zaina sits on the couch with her feet up." Nicole had her wavy auburn hair in two braids and was wearing a fuzzy sweater with leaves on it.

"You are the picture of fall," Susan said.

"Thanks! We are doing L week at school."

"That's right! You work in the office at Ida B. Wells Elementary."

Susan set the brownies down and took off her shoes. Once in her stocking feet, she followed Nicole to the living room. Zaina was on the couch, her feet clad in fuzzy pink slippers, and she was wearing a matching oversized pink sweatshirt.

"Susan, did you bring the good stuff?"

Susan held up the brown bag with the Books and Breads logo. "One dozen assorted craft brownies. Freshly made this morning!"

"It's like you brought me a little bag of heaven. This is exactly what Baby Girl and I need tonight. All my besties and brownies."

Susan walked over and gave her friend a kiss on the cheek. "How are you doing, hon?"

Zaina gave her a small smile. "Short version, I'll be okay. Long version, as soon as Devin gets out of the bathroom, we can start rant time. Did you get a drink yet? You need to have one for me and for you!"

"Sounds like a plan. I'll drink for two. You eat for two?"

Zaina patted her fuzzy belly. "You hear that? Susan is looking out for us."

"Where should I put the brownies?" Susan asked.

"As far as I am concerned you should leave them right here." Zaina held out her hands.

Susan chuckled.

Nicole said, "I'll get some plates and forks, and we can have the brownies out here, so you don't have to walk around."

"You are spoiling me, Nicole. I am allowed to walk around."

"I promised Jasper."

"Ah yes, that sounds right. Did he call you himself or did he relay it via Sean?"

"He called me."

"I don't know if I should let it go, or add it to my list for rant time," Zaina said.

"He didn't need to bother to call, because I'd be looking out for you and Baby Girl, anyway." Nicole said.

"Thanks for that. I know you've always got my back." Zaina had a grin a mile wide on her face as she finished talking, and it warmed Susan's heart to see her old friend so happy.

Devin walked into the living room and sat down in one of the two brown leather recliners. "Given that this was a total bachelor pad before you moved in, I'm surprised that Jasper didn't spring for fancy massage chairs."

"That's probably because he was hardly home before I came along. I think he slept more at the brewery than here."

"Makes sense. When I opened my law office, there were nights I slept on my office couch. There were even a few late nights when I fell asleep on my desk. Do you know how embarrassing it is to wake up with a contract stuck to your face via drool?"

Everyone laughed picturing Devin with a paper on her face.

"On that note, who's ready to try my amazing autumn sangria?" Nicole asked.

"Yes, please," said Devin.

"I'll try it," Susan said.

"What all is in it?" Zaina asked.

"I was going to look for a recipe online. Then I said to myself, Nicole, you're married to a chef. Why don't you wing it?" The girls laughed, and she continued. "Seriously though, I saw a short video and modified that recipe. It's a couple of chopped-up apples, a handful of fresh cranberries, a quart of apple cider, some cinnamon, and nutmeg. I split that in half and added one bottle of white wine to half the batch and one liter of sparking water to the other half."

Zaina said, "Thanks, babe."

"You're welcome! I hope you like the mocktail. If you do, I'm going to make a batch for everyone at work for Halloween."

Devin stretched in her seat. Her natural hair was in small braids that she had plaited into one large braid resting on her shoulder. She was wearing a yellow blouse and a pair of navy dress pants. "I should have brought sweats to change into tonight. I've been stuck in these dress clothes since six a.m."

"Did you have court today?"

Devin nodded. "Hours of sitting around to spend fifteen minutes in front of a judge."

Nicole shook her head. "One of these days, you are going to *be* the judge."

"I'll toast to that," Devin replied.

Susan had been sitting on the end of the couch, Zaina's feet in her lap, and now she moved them aside and got up. "Nicole, I'll help you with the drinks."

"That would be great."

Nicole turned and started walking down the hall to the kitchen. This was Susan's first visit to Zaina's new home with Jasper. As she followed Nicole, she looked around. She guessed it couldn't be more than five years old, based on the style of the exterior and the interior. It had all hardwood floors with gray walls and white trim. The vibes were very masculine, and Susan looked forward to the changes Zaina would make over the months and years, especially if she was right that she was having a girl.

"I made a cinnamon rimming sugar just to make the drinks extra festive. I know Zaina is nervous about pre-eclampsia and how baby Z is doing, so I wanted to do what I could to make tonight fun and normal."

"Do you have girls' nights often?"

"We try to get together monthly. It depends on Devin's schedule since she has kids, a husband who travels like crazy, and a demanding job." Nicole handed Susan a carafe. "This is the sangria with booze."

Susan took the sangria and waited as Nicole dipped a mason jar into a plate of cinnamon sugar. She turned it over and handed it to Susan who filled the glass. Once three glasses were filled, Susan put the sangria back in the fridge and took out a second carafe.

"This is the non-alcohol, right?"

Nicole looked at the container. "Yep. I put a cinnamon stick in the one without booze so I didn't mix them up."

Susan poured the mocktail into the waiting jar. They each carried two glasses into the living room, and Susan handed the mocktail to Zaina.

"Raise your glasses, girlies," Zaina said.

Susan raised her glass and looked around the room. Suddenly, her eyes began to sting. It had been too long since she'd been part of a friend group.

"A toast to my besties for keeping me sane right now."

Everyone leaned forward and clinked their glasses, then took a drink.

"Who's ready for rant time?" Zaina asked. "Should we go in order of oldest to youngest?"

"Fine by me. I've got no issues with being the oldest by one year. Y'all better get ready to help Ben throw an amazing fortieth birthday party." Devin said.

"We've got Sean's chef magic and Jasper's amazing beers. Maybe by the time your party rolls around, Susan and Donnie will be a thing, and Donnie can make the cake," Nicole said.

Devin had a half-eaten s'mores brownie on her plate. "I might do brownies instead of a cake."

"Do we have to wait a year for this party? I'm ready for a brownie bar now," Zaina said.

Nicole waved her hand above the plate of brownies on the table. "You don't need to wait. It's all right here."

Zaina laughed. "You're right. Hand me a peanut butter chocolate chunk brownie. I need protein and calcium."

Nicole handed Zaina a plate and a fork.

"Are we ready for the ranting now?" Susan asked.

"Yes, let's start. Susan, it's your first time with the group. Do you want to go first?"

Susan shook her head, "No thanks, I'd rather go last, see how this ranting works."

"Good point," said Nicole. "I'll go first. Sean is working too much. Now that he's doing catering, he's bringing home paperwork and spending a good chunk of time on his Mondays off working. He needs to listen to me and hire someone to work part-time and help with the paperwork end of the business."

"That really stinks. Why is he reluctant to hire?" Devin asked.

"I think he is worried about the expense."

"Oh! I have a potential solution! Do we do solutions or just rants?" Susan asked.

"A solution would be great," Nicole said as she cut a cherry chocolate chunk brownie and put half on her plate.

"Contact the community college and Marley Creek High School and see if there are any students that would want to intern."

The corners of Nicole's mouth turned up, "That's a great idea! Thank you, Susan!"

Devin raised her glass to Susan. "Our rant night is already better with you here. I'll go next. I'm happy to say I don't have anything to rant about this time. Even better than that, Ben has a new assignment and doesn't have to travel for a while. He's putting the twins to bed tonight while I'm here!"

Nicole got up and gave Devin a hug. "I love that for you guys!"

Devin nodded at Zaina. "Your turn."

Zaina frowned. "I hate to complain. I should probably skip."

Nicole moved over and sat next to her on the couch. She rubbed her friend's shoulder. "If something is bothering you, this is your safe space to let it out, so it doesn't sit and fester. What's going on?"

Zaina threw her head back and looked up at the ceiling. "It's Jasper. He's driving me nuts! I mean, I get it; he's worried about me and the baby. Heck, I'm worried about me and the baby. But I swear if he could wrap me up and tuck me in bed until my due date, he would! We talked to my doctor today, and she said based on my bloodwork and the symptoms, she's not worried about pre-eclampsia."

Nicole, Devin, and Susan gasped simultaneously. "That's fantastic news!" Devin said.

"I know, right? I still need to take it easy, but she said I'm off bed rest."

Nicole put her hand over her heart.

"Jasper is insisting that it would be better if I stayed on bed rest. I said to him, better for whom? Certainly not me! I'd like to go over to my shop a few days a week, and I'd like to go for a walk. It's not as if I want to go work on my feet all day or run a marathon. I just want to do things that make me feel like my old self." Zaina brushed tears from her eyes. "These damn hormones."

Nicole put her arm around Zaina. Devin moved the brownies and perched on the edge of the coffee table. She put her hand on Zaina's knee.

"I get it. When I was pregnant with the twins, Ben wanted to hire a nurse to stay with us for the last trimester. Can you imagine?"

Zaina barked out a laugh. "Devin Belmont, Esquire and mayor of Marley Creek with a nurse in tow? That's crazy!"

Susan listened to the friends and didn't comment. She could relate to not liking being coddled. She'd been controlled by her mom growing up, and she'd already divorced one man who thought he could dictate her behavior.

"It's not the same, Zaina, but I can relate. Walking helps my stress and anxiety. I would be mad if my husband didn't trust me to know if I could handle it or not. I'd feel like they were saying they knew my body better than me."

Zaina sniffed and blew her nose. "Yes, you understand. That's what I'm saying."

"We all know Jasper is crazy in love with you and ready to be the best dad he can," Nicole said. Zaina smiled and nodded. "I'm sure if you tell him how you are feeling, he'll listen."

"Girls, thanks for listening to me. I feel so much better already; group hug?"

Susan got up and joined the group hug; then she sat back down.

Nicole stood up and carried the empty glasses back to the kitchen. In less than a minute, she returned. She handed Susan a full glass. "I'm so glad you could make it tonight."

After hearing everyone else's rants, Susan felt more comfortable. "I am so happy to be here. I didn't know how badly I needed some girl time and to rant! How much time do I have?" Susan looked at the group.

"It's only seven-thirty, take all the time you need," Devin said.

"I almost had to bring my mom with me tonight. That, or I wouldn't have been able to make it at all. Zaina, when you were over visiting, she was on her best behavior. For some reason, she really loves you."

Zaina scoffed. "For some reason? Of course, she loves me. I'm delightful."

Susan took a sip of her drink. "What I mean is, she hated that we hung out in high school. She thought you ran around after boys and drank."

Zaina chuckled. "Your mom's always been so blunt. She only thought that because I was a little goth teen. I didn't date or drink that much!"

"You definitely had more fun than I did," Susan said.

Nicole said, "Oh, there is no doubt there. Zaina and I had some wild times. Remember when we ditched school and tried to reenact the Ferris Bueller movie?"

Zaina winced. "Baby Girl is kicking my ribs. I think she knows your voices and she can tell we are having a fun time."

"Aww," Devin said. "I'm sure she can hear our laughter. We can't wait to meet you, Baby Girl."

"Well, we can wait until December, Stay in there until you're fully cooked!" Nicole said.

Susan giggled and took a drink.

"Now back to Susan's rant," Devin said.

"Thanks. My mom. She's always been harsh, judgmental, and controlling. She's the main reason I went away to college and hardly ever came back to Marley Creek. Until now, anyway. She's always been a pessimist, but these days, she's just downright mean, and I can't even find caretakers to come in and give me a little break. She's basically blacklisted from Helping Hearts at this point."

Devin frowned. "My goodness, how did you find care?"

"I spent the last few days on the phone. Then I was on messenger today going back and forth with potential caregivers. I even called City Hall looking for recommendations."

"Please tell me they directed you to the resident section of the website and offered to look it up for you if you had any trouble," Devin said switching into mayor mode.

"Yes, ma'am," Susan said and continued. "I called the list on the website, but I didn't have any luck finding respite care for tonight. I was ready to give up, but then someone in the Marley Creek community group posted that they did home health care. Long story short, she could come over tonight. Downside was, it cost me two hundred and fifty dollars."

"Two hundred-fifty bucks just to hang out with us?" Zaina said.

"I was desperate. I needed this so badly. You have no idea!"

"Oh, I get it. I think I'd pay lawyer rates to spend time with my girls," Devin said.

Nicole smiled. "If we have any leftover sangria, I'll put it in a mason jar so you can take it home. It sounds like you need it the most."

"Thanks. Donnie asked me out for tomorrow afternoon, and now I'm back to square one trying to find care for my mom. It's exhausting and expensive."

Zaina asked, "What about inviting Donnie over to your mom's and having the date there?"

Susan laughed bitterly.

Zaina frowned. "Yeah, I knew that wasn't a good idea as soon as I said it out loud."

"No worries. It's sweet of you to try and think of ways to solve my problem."

Nicole tapped her glass. "I might have a solution. I can't promise anything, but—"

"I'll try anything. Well, you know, within reason."

Nicole nodded. "We have a few teacher's aides at work who do babysitting outside of school, and I think a few of them may have worked in home health. At the very least, we have some aides that also work at daycare facilities. Now I know it's not the same, but these aides have thick skins and patience for days. It might just work."

"That would be amazing. What info do you need from me?"

Nicole handed Susan her phone. "Put your contact information in my phone and I'll text them. If anyone is available, I'll pass on your number. If that's okay?"

"You've made my night. No heck, you've made my month. Please let them know if they are interested that my mom can be a blunt jerk. She makes rude comments about people's sizes, so if that is an issue, I understand. If anyone is still interested, I'll pay above the going rate, and if needed, I'll arrange transportation to and from my mom's house."

"I don't want to promise anything, but there are a couple of aides that are coming to mind who have experience and should be able to handle your mom. I'll get a hold of them first thing in the morning and tell them you need to know by lunchtime."

Susan hopped up and hugged Nicole. "I can't thank you enough! You're amazing."

"She really is!" Zaina said.

Now that the rants were over, and some solutions were available, talk moved on. The group discussed Devin's twins, Zaina's upcoming baby shower, and the high school reunion. Susan had forgotten how nice it was to be part of a circle of friends. Best of all, she might have reliable respite care. As Susan was putting on her coat to leave, Zaina asked her a question.

"Now that you have care for your mom hopefully sorted, are you excited about your date with Donnie?"

Susan zipped up her coat, and then she pulled her hair out from the back of it. She nodded. "I haven't been this excited in years!"

Chapter Twelve

♥

Donnie

Sebastian sat at the kitchen table working on his school laptop. His shoulders hunched as he typed. His hair had fallen forward, and Donnie looked at the back of his neck. It was tanned, but for a small scar near the base. Donnie remembered when Sebastian had been a toddler and had fallen down a few stairs. He closed his eyes, thinking about the look on Maggie's face when they'd rushed to the Emergency Room.

It would always be unfair that Maggie didn't get to see her son grow up, but he no longer believed if he were to go on a date or maybe even have a girlfriend that it would be dishonoring her memory. She'd always have his love, but maybe now he could find a new love, too, or at least companionship. Sebastian was beginning to make his way in the world. It was time Donnie did too.

"What are you working on?"

"I have an essay due by midnight for World History."

"Midnight?"

"We have to submit it online."

"I see. Back in my day, we had to print papers and turn them in to the teacher."

"Right. You're old, Dad, I get it," Sebastian said, looking at his screen and typing.

"Do you need any help from me before I go?"

"No." Then Sebastian turned around. He tossed back his bangs and looked at his dad. "Why are you dressed up? Where are you going? You don't go places."

"Ha, ha. I go out. Sometimes," Donnie said.

"Is that a new shirt?"

Donnie smoothed down his new navy long-sleeve shirt. He sucked in his stomach and stood tall. "Does it look okay?"

Sebastian shrugged. "It's fine. I don't know why you're standing weird. You look fine."

Donnie breathed normally. "I'll be back way before midnight, and you should have your essay done."

"Where are you going?"

Donnie paused. He scratched his beard nervously. "I'm going to meet a friend and watch some football at Jesse's."

"Oh, that's cool."

"If you need anything, just call me."

"What would I need?" Sebastian ask, going back to his laptop.

"I don't know—just saying if you did. I love you." Donnie said.

Sebastian didn't respond. Donnie was used to it.

The drive over to Susan's house was short. Susan lived on the other side of Main Street from Donnie's business and home. Marley Creek was set up in quadrants. The northwest section was bordered by Main Street and the railroad track and butted up against the forest surrounding Marley Lake. The southwest section was over the railroad tracks, and its section of Main Street included Donnie's Books and Breads as well as Zaina's shop and the pet bakery and supplies shop, Pupcakes and Clawssaints.

Donnie lived in a subdivision about a half mile from Main Street behind his shop. Susan's Mom's house was in the southeast quadrant. She lived a few blocks east of Ida B. Wells Elementary School. Jessie's Pub was on her side of Main Street. Donnie's GPS brought him to a well-maintained Cape Cod with a bay window and a small porch. The house was white and had baby blue shutters. Donnie pulled up into the driveway and turned off the car. Would Susan want him to text her and wait in the car, or should he go to the door? He didn't know what to do. Heat flooded his body and sweat broke out under his arms.

He sent her a text saying he was in the driveway and asked if he should come knock on the door. Then he stared at his phone waiting for her to respond. The song he was playing in the car finished, and she hadn't replied.

"I better just go knock on the door. Should have done that when I got here," he mumbled to himself. Donnie got out of the car and walked up the driveway. He climbed up the stairs and pressed the doorbell. Nervous energy zipped through him, so he shoved his hands in his pockets and rocked on his feet. Donnie hadn't stood on a porch waiting to pick up a girl for a date in decades. Butterflies fluttered in his stomach. How many seconds had passed since he rang the doorbell? Should he knock on the door?

The door flew open. Susan's big brown eyes shined brightly. Her cheeks were flushed, and her plump red lips were glossy. She wore a lavender wrap dress that clung to her curves over black tights and knee-high boots.

"Donnie! Come on in!" She opened the screen door and ushered him inside. He walked across the threshold into the darkened living room. In the middle was an empty medical bed. Sitting in a recliner was Dorothy, and in the wingback chair next to her was a blonde woman who looked to be around thirty years old. She was wearing an Ida B. Wells Elementary T-shirt and leggings.

Donnie stood in the foyer. Susan held out her hand and he grabbed it like it was a life preserver and he was about to sink into the ocean. He squeezed her hand.

She smiled at him. "Donnie, this is Brandee. She works with Nicole."

"Hi Brandee, nice to meet you. We're actually going to Jesse's Pub tonight. I've known Sean since he came to Marley Creek."

Brandee smiled. "Great to meet you, Donnie. I've had some of your delicious coffee cakes and sandwiches when you donated them for teacher appreciation at the school."

"Glad to hear you liked them. Are you a teacher?"

"Teacher's aide. Everything I've tried from your bakery has been amazing."

Donnie grinned.

"How come you didn't bring me a coffee cake for the morning, Donnie?" Dorothy chimed in.

"Mom, play nice," Susan admonished.

"I'm serious! And some of that coffee you serve there, too."

Donnie nodded. "Ms. Brown, I didn't think to bring anything with me tonight, and I should have."

"That's right. Didn't your mother tell you to bring a gift with when you took a lady out on a date?"

Susan rolled her eyes. "Mom, I'm practically forty."

"Doesn't matter," Dorothy said.

"I see the error of my ways. How can I make it up to you?" Donnie snapped his fingers. "Tell you what—I'll send Susan home with a coffee cake tonight."

"What about the coffee?" Dorothy rocked in the recliner; her arms crossed.

"And a bag of coffee."

Dorothy nodded. "That's what I like to hear. Now you two have fun. Brandee and I are going to play cards, right, Brandee?"

"Yes, ma'am." Brandee held up a deck of cards.

"Now that the inquisition is over, we are leaving." Susan said. She let go of Donnie's hand and took a jean jacket and her purse off the coat rack.

Donnie paused at the door. "Nice to meet you, Brandee, and have a good night, Ms. Brown."

"Call me Dorothy."

"Have a good night, Dorothy."

Dorothy waved at Donnie. Susan walked out the door and stood on the porch. Donnie shut the door behind them and clicked his key fob to unlock the doors. They walked down the steps together. When she got to the car, he followed her around and opened the door for her.

"Oh, thank you," she said.

He waited until she was seated, and then he closed the door and hustled around to his seat. Once he was in the car and started driving, he fought for something to say. The scent of her perfume filled the front seat in a pleasant way.

"So how was your day?" Susan asked him.

He turned on his blinker and relaxed. Thank goodness she was breaking the silence. "It started in the quiet that only happens in the middle of the night."

"I didn't know you were poetic. I should have surmised since you own a bookstore."

"The only indie bookstore in a thirty-mile radius," he said, then winced. This wasn't a chamber of commerce event. He was on a date.

"As someone who spent most of her childhood with her head in a book, I would have lost my mind if your store had been around back in my day. Of course, my mom wouldn't have allowed me to spend too much time there, and definitely wouldn't have funded me getting cookies and cupcakes."

"She's really hung up on food and size, huh?"

"Yep, and she hasn't mellowed much with age...but let's not talk about her. I feel like I'm with her twenty-four-seven right now."

Donnie pulled into the parking lot of Jesse's Pub. "Looks like we got the last parking spot." He got out of the car and ran around to open her door.

"You don't have to open my door," Susan said as Donnie held her door open.

"After that dressing down by Dorothy? I'm already on thin ice for not bringing a gift tonight. I better open all the doors."

Susan gave him a flirty smile and touched his arm. "Well, alright, then," she said. She slid her hand down his arm and clasped his hand. He opened the door to the restaurant and ushered her in.

A tall young woman was at the host stand holding menus. "Hi Donnie!" she said. "And oh my gosh, Susan! It's so good to see you." Mable dropped the menus on the stand and ran around to hug Susan.

Susan and Mable gave each other a rocking hug.

"I heard what happened at the university. I can't believe they did that to you!" Mable said.

Susan and Mable stepped back from their hug. "That's so sweet of you to say. The only part of my job that I miss is the mentoring. How are you doing?"

"I'm only working a couple of nights a week here and there. The internship with the kids is kicking my butt."

"I bet the kids love you, Mable," Donnie said.

Mable grinned widely. "They are the sweetest. I'm only working with the kindergarteners, so I'm lucky—little kids, little problems."

Susan nodded and Donnie noticed how she carried herself and spoke had changed. This must be what she was like at the university. Susan the mentor was sexy.

"Just remember," she said, holding Mable's hands. "You are helping them to learn how to attend and ask for what they need. These are life skills."

Mable hung on to each of Susan's words. She nodded. "Got it."

"If you need any help or just want to bounce things off me, without disclosing any specific student information, of course, call me any time; you have my cell."

Mable threw her arms around Susan again. "You're the best! First round is on me!"

"No need to do that, Mable, you're a struggling college student. I got this," Donnie said.

"Donnie, you're the best, too. Let me get you guys a table." Mable picked up the menus. "Did you two want to sit at the bar and watch the football game, or did you want to sit out here?"

Donnie looked at Susan. "What do you prefer?"

"Do you mind sitting in the dining area? You won't be able to see the TV."

Donnie's eyes flicked down Susan's body and back up to her eyes. "I don't care about the game."

"Okay, a nice table away from some of the crowd," Mable said. She led them to a small table next to the fireplace. "How's this?"

"Perfect," Donnie said.

Mable placed their menus in front of each of them and poured glasses of water from the bottle on the table. "Your waitress will be right over to take your drink orders. It was so good to see you, Susan."

"You too, Mable."

Mable walked away from the table and Donnie took a drink of water. His mouth was dry.

"So, ah, have you been here before?"

Susan shook her head. "I haven't."

"Everything Sean makes is delicious. We're lucky to have him here in Marley Creek. He could be the head chef at one of the five-star restaurants downtown."

The waitress came by and took their drink order. Susan got a white wine, and Donnie went with a lager. He swallowed around a lump in his throat as he searched for something to say.

Susan toyed with a pendant on a gold chain. He followed her hand and his eyes were drawn to her voluptuous breasts. She was a goddess. His mouth was dry again.

"So why did you decide to open a bakery that sells books?" she asked.

His heartbeat slowed and he took a breath. A runner dropped off their drink orders.

He closed his eyes as he took a long pull from his frosted glass. "It was going to be just a bakery, but Maggie did the market research and suggested we add on a bookstore."

"And the rest was history?"

"Pretty much." Donnie smiled wistfully.

He raised his glass and Susan raised hers, "Cheers," he said.

"Cheers," she repeated, and they took a drink. Donnie's eyes lingered on the curve of her neck. He could see her pulse beating and he imagined putting his lips to it, kissing her at her pulse point and then moving down until he was swirling his tongue around the nipples he could see pressing against her dress.

The waitress came by to take their order.

"I'll go with butternut squash ravioli with the brown sage sauce," Susan said.

"And for you, sir?" the waitress asked, turning to Donnie.

Donnie paused. He really wanted a burger, but he should be watching his cholesterol and trying to lose a few pounds.

"You should get the burger. It looks amazing," Susan said, nodding toward a server carrying a cheeseburger on a brioche bun with a side of hand-cut French fries.

Donnie decided that was a sign. "You read my mind." He addressed the waitress. "I'll take a Jessie Burger with American cheese and for the side, give me the mixed greens salad."

"What dressing would you like?"

"The vinegarette."

The waitress repeated their order and walked away.

"Thanks for mentioning the burger. I haven't had one in a long time. I was debating whether to get it or try one of the under six hundred calorie dinners."

"You're welcome. I hope I made a good choice for you." She chuckled.

"If it's half as good as I remember, I'll be happy." Donnie took a deep breath. "I need to be upfront with you."

Susan paused and set down her wine. "Go on."

"This is the most dating I've done since she's been gone. Part of me will always miss her, but I feel ready to enter a new chapter of my life. Sebastian will be going to college in a couple of years. My business is an established cornerstone of our town. I think it's time that I think about myself. But I don't have a clue how things work these days with dating. How soon should I text you after tonight? Do I assume we are dating other people? Do I ask if you are on the apps?"

Susan reached across the table and held his hand. The soft skin of her palm against his soothed him. He waited for her to answer, and he didn't think he could find a better person to navigate this new dating world with.

"I think it's fair for you to start thinking about your needs. If you don't, you might be awfully lonely when Sebastian leaves for college. You can text me whenever you'd like. If I don't answer, I'm probably busy with Mom, either helping her with something or stuck in a medical office with bad Wi-Fi. I barely have time to breathe most days, let alone be on an app or find time to date multiple people."

Donnie felt lighter than he'd felt in quite some time. Maybe dating could be fun. A group of boys wearing Marley Creek High football jerseys passed their table, talking and jostling each other.

"Sometimes I feel like I'm nearly a hundred years old, and other days, I feel like I was in high school last week," he said.

"Did you play football back then?"

"I did. I grew up in the suburbs of Minneapolis. Our team was never very good, and I barely got on the field, but we had a blast. There were team pasta dinners, pep rallies, and the parties after the games. Heck, sometimes we'd all pile in a few cars and drive out to the country and drag race. And of course, there were dates out at the local make-out spot. It used to be a drive-in theater in my hometown."

"Ah yes. Do kids still go to Marley Lake?" Susan asked.

Donnie nodded. "You must have had your share of parties and boys in high school. Am I out with a former homecoming queen?"

Susan burst out laughing. Just then, their food arrived. They were silent as the food was set on the table. Once the food runner left, Susan replied.

"My high school days were filled with going to school and coming home. Unless there was an afterschool choir activity."

"Really?" Donnie raised an eyebrow. "Were you shy back then?"

Susan shook her head. "Nothing like that, I will say I have more confidence now. Back then it was my mother who prevented me from having any of those fun high school moments. She was very strict. I wanted to audition for the school musical, and she wouldn't let me. Said there were too many kids who were a bad influence." Susan paused and took a sip of her wine and then she continued, "Her opinion was the drama club kids were the ones engaging in the most sex and kids in sports did all the drinking. I was in choir because that was the only extracurricular she approved of. Well, that and debate club, but I had no interest in that. I used all my debating energy trying to get my mom to let me go on field trips. She wouldn't even let me get a part-time job. School was my full-time job."

"That must have been rough."

Susan stabbed her ravioli and brought it to her mouth. She chewed, and her narrowed eyes widened, and her shoulders relaxed. "This sage sauce is divine. You were not kidding about the food here."

"Sean deserves a Michelin star." Donnie took a bite of his burger.

Susan ate for another minute and then she spoke again. "My high school years were a slog. The only bright spot was having Zaina as my best friend. And Nicole was a pretty good friend, too. Once she got her license, she drove me to school so I could finally stop taking the bus. You see, my mom wouldn't even let me do driver's ed. I had to wait until I was eighteen."

Donnie shifted in his seat. His ears were hot and he knew they had turned bright red. His situation was very different from Susan and her mother's. Sebastian was allowed to participate in any activities he wanted as long as his grade point average was at least a B. He kept quiet.

"As soon I graduated, I was out of here. Went to college and didn't look back."

"Until now," he said.

Susan took a drink of her wine. "Did I mention that this wine pairs perfectly with my dinner? We're going to have to leave the waitress a huge tip. This is the best dinner I've had in I don't know when. I need to start coming here more often."

"I'll come with you anytime."

"Aww, thank you." She smiled. "So yeah, everything was great until the college decided to close our whole department, and it's not like any of us were given the opportunity to move into another department. No, instead they told us we were gone at the end of the summer semester."

"That sounds awful."

"If I think about all the hours of my own time I put in to that job, it makes me nauseous. And if that wasn't enough, just as I was trying to figure out my career, I got a phone call at three in the morning that my mom was rushed to the hospital with a broken hip."

Donnie pushed aside his finished plate. "No good calls happen after two a.m."

"Right?" Susan hit the table with her hand. "It turned out that my mom had fallen down her stairs. She's lucky she didn't break her neck, because when they did x-rays, they found she has advanced osteoporosis. She was on the floor for hours before she managed to push herself over to the phone and call for help. She almost died."

"That sounds overwhelming."

"I'm sorry—am I talking too much? It's just haven't dated in ages. I think I'm out of practice. I feel like I'm a lot for a first date," Susan said.

"If we look at it like this is our third date, then I don't think you are talking too much at all."

"You are the sweetest man."

Donnie blushed. "And that's how you wound up back in Marley Creek?"

She nodded. "It's funny—I spent my teen years trapped under my mom's thumb feeling suffocated and resentful, and now here I am back under her roof with a curfew and limited options to leave the house."

"Sometimes things repeat in ways you could not imagine. If this situation was happening to a friend of yours, what would you say to them?"

Susan's mouth was agape. "Did you minor in psychology?"

"No, I've got a basic degree in business administration, but I do spend a lot of time helping customers at the bakery and bookstore. Sometimes I learn a lot about a person when they need book recommendations."

"You ask them what books they'd recommend to a friend and go from there?"

Donnie pointed at Susan. "Exactly."

"If I was talking to Zaina, I'd tell her it sounded like the Universe had brought her back to work on her relationship with her mother before it was too late, and she had regrets."

"And if it wasn't Zaina, our favorite witch?"

"I'd say that they could have decided not to come home, so they should spend some time uncovering why they chose to return to their hometown and move back in with a parent they'd been distant with for many years. Do I get a book recommendation now?"

Donnie chuckled. "I feel like you don't need any book recs on this topic, but if you want a cozy mystery or some romantic suspense, hit me up."

"I might do that. So now that we've psychoanalyzed me, how can we work on you?"

"Just being here is how I'm working on me."

The waitress stopped at their table. "Do we need any boxes?"

Susan raised her hand. "I'll take one."

"Can I get you two another round of drinks or dessert?"

Donnie looked at Susan, "Did you want anything? I'm driving."

Susan shook her head. "I'm sorry, I don't have any room left. The ravioli was amazing."

The waitress smiled. "I'll be right back with the check and a box."

"Great," Donnie said.

Donnie's heart rate was rising again. Dinner was over, and he hoped she wasn't ready to end the evening. It was just past nine. "D-do you have to get home now? Or should we go get a nightcap?" He winced. She'd just said she didn't want another drink.

Susan pushed her hair behind her ear. The waitress dropped off the box and the check. Donnie snatched up the check to avoid any doubt he was going to pay.

"I can help with the check."

Donnie shook his head. "No. I got this. Besides, you're not working. I mean, you are working harder than you probably did at Illinois State, but you aren't getting paid. Does that make sense?"

Susan smiled and bobbed her head. "Yes, it does. Thank you. It's very sweet of you."

Donnie's stomach clenched. He didn't want her to think he was too sweet. He was going for brawny, sexy almost-knight in shining armor.

"I don't have to rush home. What did you have in mind?"

An idea hit Donnie. "Let's go make out at Marley Lake," he blurted.

He pulled out his wallet and covered the bill, plus a nice tip in cash. The waitress walked by and took the bill.

"You're serious?" Susan raised an eyebrow.

"I can't help everything going on with your mom, but I can help you have a little fun." They stood. He put his palm on her lower back, and they quickly left Jesse's Pub.

Once they were in the car, she cupped his face and kissed him on the mouth. "There will be more of that once we're parked at the lake."

He revved the engine, "Let's go!"

"Are you giving me high school Donnie?" she asked.

He ran a hand through his hair. "Imagine all this gray hair is dark brown and I have no beard—not even a little straggly mustache."

"I still would have found you swoony. Did you bake back then?"

"I made chocolate chip cookies for my teammates on Fridays before games. Spirit Cookies; the guys loved them." The corners of his mouth turned up. "I haven't thought about that in years."

Donnie pulled into the Marley Lake parking area. He turned on the radio. "When did you graduate from high school?"

"Two thousand and four."

"Wait, so this year is your twentieth class reunion?"

"Yep."

"You're a baby! I graduated last century. Class of nineteen ninety-seven."

"You look much too young to be that old," She joked.

Donnie parked the car and turned on the radio. He clicked through radio stations until he found the Early Aughts satellite radio station. "This Love" by Maroon 5 filled the car.

"If you're trying to nail my senior year vibes, all I need is a skinny scarf and a pair of fake Uggs."

"My crush on you would have been legendary." He brushed his knuckles against her cheek.

Chapter Thirteen

♥

Susan

Susan body was vibrating. Donnie's knuckles slid down from her cheek. He held her chin and then he closed the gap between his lips and hers. His kiss was feather soft. She pressed her lips to his. She couldn't help but suck on his bottom lip. When she released it, his tongue pressed against her lips. She opened her mouth, eager to taste him. At first, he was tentative, lightly stroking, and she moaned. Their tongues tangled together. Warmth spread low in her belly. She rubbed her legs together to try to relieve some of the pressure. Donnie broke the kiss off and moved lower, kissing her jaw. Her senses were filled with him. She wanted to be closer to him and regretted that they were in the front seat of his SUV. Susan tugged off her cardigan.

"Do you want me to stop?" Donnie said against her throat.

"God, no."

She finished pulling off her cardigan. She laid it down on the center console and leaned across it.

"Wait, I've got a better idea," Donnie said, "if you're comfortable with it."

"What are you thinking? You're the car make-out expert here. I've honestly never done this," Susan said.

Donnie eyes widened. "You've never messed around in a car?"

"I didn't do anything until I went away to college, and we didn't have cars as freshmen. If we were in a dorm room, then I could show you some things."

Donnie burst out into a big belly laugh. "I'm going to hold you to that." He moved his seat back as far as it would go and then he tapped his thighs. "Come over here."

Susan awkwardly crawled over until she was straddling his lap. She felt the wetness of her panties. Her tights were a thin barrier between her core and the jeans holding back his cock. She rocked back and forth a little, enjoying the friction. She looked down into Donnie's eyes. Even in the low light, she could see his desire. He pushed back her hair and took her face in his hands. He kissed her long and hard. With each stroke of his tongue, electricity built within her. She wished they were not in a car, but on a couch or a bed, or even just in the backseat. She took Donnie's hand and placed it on her breast.

He raised his other hand and palmed her breast. "You have a gorgeous body."

Susan felt her cheeks redden. She'd always had a hard time taking any compliments, especially if they were about her body. "Thank you," she said and went back to kissing him. "Kind of regretting this wrap dress right about now," she added as he rolled her pebbled nipple between his thumb and forefinger.

"We can make it work," he said. He cupped her breast, pulling her toward him. He took her nipple in his mouth through her dress. She was so glad she'd worn a barely-there lace bra.

"God your tongue is amazing! The friction," she gasped. She needed to grind against him.

He stopped sucking and said, "If you keep up what you're doing, I'm going to come in my pants like we're back in high school."

"Is that supposed deter me?" She pressed down on his zipper.

He made a guttural sound in his throat. "Are we really doing this?"

"I don't want to stop. Do you?"

"I-I don't." He put his hands on her ass and squeezed.

"That feels good," she moaned.

She bore down, stroking across him. He moved his hands to her hips, pushing her back and forth across his jean encased cock. She caught his mouth, and they started kissing again. Soon she was swallowing his moans, and she was so close. "Faster," she begged and bucked against him.

"Yes, fuck yes," he said.

She cupped her breast, rubbing her nipple with her thumb. He watched as she touched herself and the heat in his eyes tore through her. She was so close. He nipped at her bottom lip and grabbed her ass, pressing her against him.

"You are incredible," he whispered, and that tipped her over. The words, his strong hands around her, and the heady smell of them in the close confines of the car had done things to her.

He rubbed his hands up and down her back. It was so soothing she was certain she could fall asleep right there. She closed her eyes and allowed herself to relax for a few minutes. Donnie kissed her head.

"If this is a taste of what I missed in high school, I have a lot to catch up on."

"I'm here to help. Just let me know what we should do next," Donnie said.

A phone alarm sounded from the passenger's seat. Susan lifted her head. "Shoot—that's my fifteen-minute warning. I've got to get home."

"We don't want to break curfew. I want to stay on your mom's good side."

"But I feel bad. I hate to leave you, ah, unfulfilled."

"You could make it up to me next time?" Donnie helped Susan off his lap and back onto the passenger seat.

"Most definitely," Susan said. They both adjusted their clothing.

Susan was still feeling weak in the knees. Donnie reached across the console. She gripped his hand. She'd been feeling overwhelmed and adrift for months, and now her reserves had been restored.

"Yes, don't make my mom mad. Trust me on that."

"Noted," Donnie said.

They drove to Books and Breads so Donnie could run in and get the promised coffee and coffee cake for Dorothy. After the quick stop, Donnie drove toward Susan's house. "When can I see you again?" Donnie said.

"That depends," she said, keeping her voice light, so he'd know she was kidding.

"On what?" he asked. His voice matched her tone.

"Can you top this date? I feel twenty years younger."

"The high school has a home game this week. How would you like to go to the football game with me?"

He pulled into Susan's driveway and put the car in park.

"I'd love to. It's a date," she said. "And I didn't forget I owe you one!" She winked and gave him a quick kiss on the cheek. Then she hopped out of the car with the goods for Dorothy.

Chapter Fourteen

♥

Donnie

Donnie wasn't normally one to whistle while he worked, but ever since his date the other day with Susan he couldn't help humming, whistling or smiling so wide his cheeks hurt. His phone chimed. It was a text from Susan.

SUSAN: Are we pre-gaming before the game?

DONNIE: (shrug emoji) In high school I was always on the field. I never got to pregame.

SUSAN: I heard these days people sneak stuff in their big metal water bottles.

DONNIE: They probably do, but since my son is in the marching band, I've never drank before or during the game.

SUSAN: Scratch that idea. Maybe we can just make out under the bleachers?

DONNIE: (kissing face emoji)

SUSAN: (heart eyes emoji)

Donnie tucked his phone into his pocket. He put on a new pair of gloves and started making lunch orders. Jasper Kane, owner of Hop's Heaven and Zaina's husband, was coming in to pick up a mixed bagel sandwich tray with chips and a box of Books and Breads Java for his weekly staff meeting. Donnie appreciated that Jasper always chose to order from one of Marley Creek's local restaurants instead of giving his business to big chains.

That's what made Marley Creek work: local businesses and residents who made the choice to support each other. That and the fact they had a train station, making it easy for anyone from the city to come out for one of the town festivals or the annual marathon.

It also helped Donnie to book authors to do signings at his store. The convenience of the commute plus the book cover cookies he made for each event had made his little store a destination for even New York Times best-selling authors. That reminded him, he needed to order books for the October Brownies Book Club. This month they were reading a new paranormal cozy mystery featuring an amateur sleuth who was a vampire. He'd check with Jasper and Sean from Jesse's Pub for a signature drink for book club night.

Donnie finished packing the food for Jasper just as Jasper walked into Books kand Breads. "Hey Buddy, how's it going?"

Jasper took off his sunglasses and ran a hand through his shoulder-length dark hair. He had circles under his brown eyes. "Can I get a red eye? I didn't sleep for shit last night."

"Coming right up. Do you have time to talk? Or do you need it to go?"

Jasper checked his phone. "Put it in a regular mug. It tastes better that way. I've got some time."

"Did you eat anything today?"

"Shit, I forgot to eat," Jasper said.

Donnie chuckled to himself. He didn't understand how anyone could forget a meal, but he'd realized Jasper sometimes was so focused on other things that he didn't stop to take a break.

"Do you want something now, or are you going to wait until you get to work and eat with your staff?"

Jasper shook his head. "Nah, I'm good."

Donnie crossed his arms. "You need to eat."

"I promise I'll have a bagel and a brownie when I get back to Hop's." Jasper snapped his fingers. "Speaking of food, I need some of your brownies for Zaina."

"What kind does she want? I have s'mores, peanut butter chocolate chunk, and raspberry swirl left."

Jasper tapped his chin. "Better give me a half dozen, two of both."

Donnie opened a box and used a pair of tongs to put the brownies inside. Then he closed and taped the cellophane windowed box shut. Donnie added the box to one of Jasper's bags. He refilled his own cup of coffee and sat down across from Jasper. "What's going on?"

"I don't know how I'm going to make it until the baby is born."

"Is Zaina okay? I think Susan mentioned she doesn't need bed rest?"

"She's good! She's off the bed rest. It looks like pre-eclampsia isn't an issue."

Donnie put his hand on his chest. "That's fantastic news, Jasp!"

"I know. It's really great news, but she still needs to take it easy. Which reminds me: I need to ask a favor."

"Is it daily brownie delivery?"

No, not that. It's the Haunted Hayride fundraiser. We signed up to be one of the vignettes."

"Oh yeah? What were you going to play?"

"I was going to be Lestat from *Interview with a Vampire* and Zaina was going to be a buxom vixen circa the French Revolution era."

"Gotcha. So, do you need me to dress up and play the vixen?" Donnie waggled his eyebrows.

Jasper pretended to think about it. "Or, maybe you and Susan could take our place? It's not until next weekend, so you have time to decide how you'd want to play it. You look more like the werewolf type. I suggest you keep it simple. You're a werewolf and she's a damsel in distress, or she could be Little Red Riding Hood and you're the big, bad werewolf. Once the hayride goes past, you leave your spot and chase it around the corner and that's about all you have to do."

"That sounds like a blast. Put us down for that."

"Are you two officially an 'us' now?"

"We haven't had a relationship talk yet, but I'm sure she'd be up for volunteering, and it's for a good cause."

"Cool, thanks for the help, man."

"If Zaina is okay, why are you not getting sleep?"

"Do you have any idea how much stuff you must get done to have a baby? I was up until two a.m. putting together a cradle. Assembling furniture is not my forte, let me tell you. And then, right when I was about to fall asleep, my gorgeous wife started snoring. I think the neighbor's dog heard it and started howling."

Donnie started laughing halfway through Jasper's description of his evening, and by the time Jasper finished, Donnie had tears streaming down his face. Jasper shook his head and started laughing, too.

"Dude, you're going to be a great dad, and you don't have to do it by yourself. I'll come over and help you with the furniture or if you need painting done. As far as Zaina's snoring, if she's asleep, go sleep on the couch or in your guest room. She'll probably be grateful to have the bed to herself. Maggie snored and tossed and turned like crazy in her last trimester. It worked out for us. She'd stay up later and sleep in and I'd go to bed at eight at night and get up at three."

"I should get used to the lack of sleep. When our daughter arrives, all hope of sleep will be gone."

"It's not as bad as you think, and those days go by so fast. It's actually easier when they're babies. One day you'll turn around and your little angel who cried when you had to go to work will be in high school and giving you the silent treatment."

"Are things rough with your kiddo right now?"

Donnie frowned. "He used to light up when he saw me. Now it's like a rolling shutter comes down over his face."

"Man, I'm sorry. Do you think it's because you're dating Susan?"

Donnie's face burned, "I, uh, haven't told Sebastian about Susan yet."

Jasper pursed his lips and side-eyed Donnie.

Donnie's cheeks flamed.

"Dude," Jasper said.

"I know! You're right, I need to talk to him. I'm planning to do it tonight."

"It's your business, but yeah, you should really let him know you are dating. If he isn't upset about that, what's going on with him?"

"From talking to other parents at band practice pick up, I'd say we are all going through it. But Sebastian has been very mad at me since I haven't signed off on him doing student driving."

"Really? How come?" Jasper paused, and Donnie could see light dawning in his eyes. "Oh, because of Maggie. Sorry, the caffeine hasn't kicked in yet. I'm an idiot."

"Yes, of course, that's part of it, but it's not like I get freaked out when he's in a car and I'm not driving. This is solely because I don't think he is mature enough to get behind the wheel of a car."

Jasper's brow furrowed. He took a sip of his coffee. It looked to Donnie like Jasper had something to say. Donnie clenched his jaw. He didn't want to argue with his friend about what it was like to have your only son out in the world. But Jasper didn't say anything. Instead, he looked at his watch.

"Shit, I've got to get to work." He chugged the rest of his coffee and stood.

"Thanks again for the order and give Zaina my best."

"I will," Jasper said. He picked up his order, adjusting the bags so he could make it out to his car.

"I'll get the door for you." Donnie rushed over to the door and pressed the auto open button.

"I hope things get better with Sebastian."

"I hope you get some sleep."

"You and me both," Jasper said, and then he was out the door.

Anxiousness filled Donnie as he spent the rest of his work day doing routine tasks while his mind ran through various scenarios. Would Sebastian even care that he was dating someone? It seemed highly unlikely that he'd be completely fine with his father dating for the first time in his life. Looking back, Donnie realized that he might have done more harm than good by trying to wait until his son went to college to date. It would have been easier on Sebastian if Donnie had done some dating over the years.

Too late. Now Donnie would have to hope for the best, or not date Susan. His stomach roiled. Nope. Life without Susan was not an option now.

Donnie closed the store and walked out to his car. He was going to pick up a pepperoni and peppers pizza from Best Pizza Near Me, Sebastian's favorite. He wasn't above trying to get on his son's good side before dropping a potential bombshell on a school night.

It wasn't long before Donnie was at home setting the table and tossing a salad to accompany the thick-crust pizza. He treated himself to a pumpkin ale in a bid to calm his nerves and waited for Sebastian to come home on the activity bus after marching band practice. Donnie unlocked his phone to text Susan. He clicked on her contact and began typing, "How was your day?" but then he backspaced out of the text. He didn't want to start texting Susan when Sebastian would be home at any moment.

The look on Jasper's face when he'd admitted he hadn't told Sebastian he was dating yet filled him with shame. How embarrassing. He was a grown man afraid to talk to his son. That needed to change.

The front door opened, and Donnie heard the sound of his son dropping his heavy backpack on the tile floor of the entryway.

"I got pizza," Donnie said.

"Did you get it like I like or your way?" Sebastian shouted up the stairs of the split-level ranch.

"Sebastian Style."

"Good, I'm starving and it's Bastian."

Sebastian walked over to the dining table and sat down. He placed his phone next to his plate. He had one AirPod in and started piling pizza on his plate.

"Can you go wash up first?"

"Right, sorry," Sebastian mumbled and left the table. Instead of going to the bathroom he went into the kitchen and used the sink in there. As far as Donnie was concerned, any handwashing was better than none at this point.

Donnie sipped on his beer and picked at his salad. He was too nervous to eat. Sebastian sat back down at the table. He started wolfing down food with his eyes on his phone and his hair hanging forward, covering his face. Donnie wished he could skip this conversation. He also wished Susan was here to help him, but that wasn't her place.

They were just dating; she wasn't part of this family. It had been only him and Sebastian for as long as Sebastian could remember, and if that was going to change down the road, Donnie needed to be upfront and honest with his son, starting now.

"Sebastian." Donnie looked at his son, trying to make eye contact through the mop of dark black hair. Sebastian kept eating and watching his phone.

Donnie raised his voice. "Sebastian!"

"One sec," Sebastian said through a mouthful of pizza.

Donnie crossed his arms and waited. Sebastian tapped his phone and then ran a hand through his hair.

"What's up? Did you change your mind about letting me drive?" Sebastian looked at him, and the hope Donnie could hear in his voice made his heart hurt. But he needed to stick to his guns. Sebastian was not ready to drive. If he let him try, someone could get hurt.

"It's not about that. I wanted to talk to you about a decision I made."

Sebastian crossed his arms and looked at his father. "What else are you going to tell me I can't do?"

Donnie sighed and tugged on his beard. "It's nothing like that. Would you just listen to me?"

"Fine, what is it?" Sebastian's mouth was a straight line, his eyes dull.

"I'm dating someone."

Sebastian eyebrows knit together. His face looked like he had just taken a big gulp of spoiled milk. "You're dating someone? Really?"

"Her name is Susan, she's friends with Zaina, Jasper's wife. We've gone out a couple of times and I think we'll be going out more, so I wanted to make sure you knew I was dating and see if you'd mind meeting her?"

Sebastian put his elbow on the table and his chin on his hand. "Is she your girlfriend?"

"W-we haven't decided anything like that," Donnie stuttered.

"Are you going to?"

"I—guess? I don't know. We haven't discussed it."

"Do you think she wants to meet me? Doesn't sound like she's super invested in you."

"She likes me!" Donnie felt suddenly defensive and as soon as he spoke, he wished he could take the words back. This wasn't how the conversation was supposed to go. "Look, the point is, I'm dating, and if you don't mind, I'd like you to meet her."

"Is it going to be a whole thing where she comes over for dinner?"

"No," Donnie said quickly scrapping his family dinner night idea. "We're going to the football game on Friday. I thought I could introduce you both before the game. No big deal—just a quick introduction, and then we'll go sit down and cheer you on."

Sebastian was quiet. He took a bite of his salad and chewed it while he was thinking. "Okay, that doesn't sound too bad."

Donnie relaxed in his chair. This had gone better than the driving conversation. Could it be Sebastian was maturing?

Maybe he had been selling his son short. Sebastian, having assumed the conversation was over, was back on his phone, hair back in his eyes. Earbuds in his ears.

Donnie guessed he should be happy they'd had a three-minute talk, and no one had called the other a name or left the table in a huff. Maybe this was the start of something better. Would the meeting between Susan and Sebastian go well at the football game? Acid churned in his stomach, Donnie was unsure how much of that was because of the heavy pizza dinner or anxiety.

Chapter Fifteen

♥

Susan

Susan was rummaging through her moving boxes in the damp, spider-friendly basement. It was getting colder out, and she needed to get out her fall and winter clothes. Hopefully, by winter, her mom would be back on her feet and Susan could move on with her life.

Donnie's face when he was giving her a kiss goodbye after their date flashed in her mind. Could moving on with her life mean staying in Marley Creek? Did she want to do that? And what would she do for a living? It was too soon to tell; she couldn't base her life on a few dates, even if he made her feel like gooey mush every time he caressed her cheek or kissed her on the forehead.

Energy zinged through her just thinking about their date later today. She hadn't gone to a football game in high school, and now, not only was she going, but she had a handsome football player as her date. Susan couldn't keep the smile off her face. The caretaking of her mother was draining. The time with Donnie, especially his focus on giving her the fun high school experiences she didn't have back then, filled her with happiness. Maybe she would go to the reunion.

She put another long-sleeve shirt on a hanger. Her phone buzzed. The display showed Zaina dressed up as a witch for last year's Halloween. Susan put down the arm full of clothes she was holding and brushed dust off an old kitchen table chair. She sat down and answered the call.

"Hey what's up?" Susan asked.

"Not much. I just wanted to call and thank you for taking my place at the Haunted Hayride!"

"What are you talking about?"

"You know, Jasper told me Donnie agreed you and him would take our place as actors next weekend, since I can't be standing or running around outside like I thought I'd be able to."

"Wait. Donnie signed us up to participate?"

"Y'all didn't talk about it?" Zaina asked.

"This is news to me." Susan clenched her teeth.

"Maybe I misunderstood, and Jasper meant that Donnie was going to ask you about it?"

Susan pinched the bridge of her nose. Had Donnie committed her to an event without discussing it with her first? She hoped not; she didn't like anyone making decisions on her behalf.

"I'll be seeing him later today, so I'll find out what is going on."

"Crap, I'm sorry. I don't want to cause any trouble."

"Z, you don't have anything to apologize for. I'll talk to him, and we'll figure it out."

"I was really excited that you two were going to take our place. If you were willing to dress up for the hayride fundraiser, I figured that meant you'd be coming to the class reunion for sure."

"I might do the hayride, but I'm still a no on the reunion."

"I've still got just over a month to convince you to go!" Zaina said in a sing-song tone.

"I'll talk to you later," she replied. Zaina ended the call, and Susan went back to unpacking and sorting clothes. After a while, Susan checked her phone. Donnie would be here in less than an hour, and she still needed to shower.

She started a decaf pot of coffee for her mother in the kitchen. Dorothy's favorite drink was coffee. She used to drink the real stuff all day. At least now she'd finally dialed it back and switched to decaf once dinnertime rolled around. Susan thought she should text Donnie and ask him if he could bring them a bag of coffee. Dorothy had really enjoyed the Books and Breads blend. The doorbell rang.

"Suzy, can you get the door? It's probably Brandee. I hope she brought the game she was talking about. Did you remember to put some diet cola in the fridge for her? That's what she liked to drink."

The corners of Susan's mouth ticked up. That was the most her mother had said all day. "Yep, I put a couple of cans in the fridge this morning, so they'd be nice and cold for Brandee."

"Oh good, good."

Susan opened the door. "Come on in."

Brandee walked into the Cape Cod and took off her Crocs at the front door. She was wearing a plaid brown and cream-colored flannel jacket over a pair of leggings and a big sweatshirt that said "Pumpkin Spice and Everything Nice." In one hand, she had a pink metal cup with stickers on it, and over her shoulder was a tote bag.

"Hi, Ms. Brown!" she said, and waved to Dorothy.

Dorothy smiled. Susan blinked quickly. Now her mother was smiling? Maybe her mom was turning a corner, or maybe this was a fluke. For now, Susan wasn't going to look a gift horse in the mouth.

Brandee walked over and sat down in the chair next to Dorothy's recliner. "I brought the game we talked about. She opened her tote bag and pulled out a white rectangular box that read 'Sequence.'"

Dorothy clapped her hands together. "Years ago, decades ago at this point, we played that game. Me and some of the girls would get together. They'd complain about their husbands, and I'd give them my sympathies and then we'd play for money. Are we betting tonight?"

"No thank you, Dorothy!" Brandee laughed.

"If you don't need anything from me, I'm going to head upstairs and get ready for my date."

"We're good, aren't we?" Brandee said, looking at Dorothy for confirmation.

"Yes, we are." Dorothy looked over her glasses at her daughter. "You're not wearing that, are you?"

Susan frowned. There was the mom she knew. She shook her head and walked up the stairs to get ready for her date. As she showered, she pondered what Zaina had said. She hoped there had been a misunderstanding, and not that Donnie had spoken for her. She scrubbed her elbows harder as she thought about it.

In short order, she'd put her hair up in a ponytail and applied makeup. Her phone buzzed in her back pocket. Donnie texted that he was on his way. Susan hustled downstairs. She grabbed her jean jacket off the coat rack and laced up her brown ankle boots.

"Those boots are super cute," Brandee said.

"You focus on her boots, and I'm going to figure out how to stop you. Don't think I don't see you've got two paths to a sequence right now." Dorothy said.

Brandee chuckled and shook her head.

Susan opened the door. Donnie stood on the porch holding a bag with the Books and Breads logo. "Did you bring that for me?"

"Actually, it's for your mom."

Susan smiled; even better. She took Donnie's hand and led him into the living room, where Dorothy was staring at the board game, plotting her move.

"Mom," Susan said.

Dorothy looked up. Donnie walked over and handed Dorothy the bag.

"Is this for me?"

"Yes, ma'am."

"No need to be formal, but I like it," Dorothy said.

Susan squeezed Donnie's hand. "What did he bring you?"

She pulled out a bag of coffee. Dorothy put it up to her nose and sniffed. "I'd like to have some of this right now, but I'll be up all night if I do."

"Check the bag again. I think you'll be happy." Donnie said.

Dorothy reached back into the bag and pulled out a second bag of coffee. This one had a big green label that said decaf.

"You're all right, Donnie Larson. This is much better than a bag of sugary stuff."

Susan rolled her eyes. Her mom was gifted in the art of being a buzzkill. "Geez Louise, just say thank you."

"Would you mind dumping out the coffee in the kitchen and making a fresh pot of this?" Dorothy asked Brandee holding up the coffee Donnie brought.

"Can I trust you with the game board? No cheating, Missy." Brandee wagged her finger at Dorothy and got up to make the coffee.

"We'd better head out. The game is going to start soon. If you need anything, just call me or text me or have Brandee text me, okay?" Susan gave her mom a careful hug. She felt the sharpness of her mother's bones and wished she could get her mom to enjoy food just enough to build some muscle. She was going to need it if she was going to start walking again soon. But that was a problem for another day. Tonight, she was going to enjoy Donnie's company and the simple pleasure of a small-town high school football game.

Susan followed Donnie out to his car. He ran around to open the passenger door for her. Before she got into the car, Donnie placed his hand on her hips and spun her toward him. She gasped in delight as he kissed her like he'd been overseas for weeks and finally back on solid ground. He broke off the kiss. She held on to the door, trying to regain her equilibrium. "What was that for?"

Donnie shrugged. "Just wanted you to know how much I've missed you."

"Damn," Susan said. They hadn't even left the driveway, and her nipples ached already. "This is going to be a fun night."

He didn't seem to be the kind of guy that would make plans for both of them without asking her first, but she needed to know for sure. She'd ask him about it soon.

"Yes, it is," Donnie agreed. He put the car in drive, and they headed south to Marley Creek High School.

The parking closest to the football field was already full, so they pulled into the parking lot of St. John's, the Lutheran church across from the school. Donnie pulled a couple of orange and blue seat cushions out of his backseat.

"Seat cushions, oh that's smart. I haven't been to a football game in ages, but I still remember the bleachers aren't comfortable at all." Susan said.

Donnie offered his free hand to Susan, who took it. "It gets pretty chilly once the sun goes down. I don't want that cute butt of yours to get frostbite."

Susan blushed.

A steady stream of people were walking toward the football game. Susan could see that both teams were on the field practicing. Warmth filled her chest, and she let out a shaky breath.

"Is everything okay?" Donnie asked, stopping to look at her.

Susan leaned in and gave him a hug. Her eyes stung. "I'm just really happy."

Donnie tucked the seat cushions under his arm and tilted her head up. He placed a soft kiss on her lips. She wrapped her arms around him and kissed him back hard. Then she returned to his side, and they started walking again. "It's been rough trying to find someone to watch Mom, and I'm blown away by how great Brandee is with her. She needs to go into nursing or get her teaching degree. She has more patience than anyone I know."

Donnie squeezed her hand. They got in line at the ticket booth. He let go of her hand and took out his wallet.

"You should let me pay for something," Susan said.

Donnie waved her off. "Not happening."

"Thank you," she said. Donnie handed over the money and they took turns holding out their hands to get stamped. Susan looked around at all the people sporting Marley Creek Hawks T-shirts, sweatshirts, and hats. "I should have stopped at the hardware store and bought a team shirt."

Donnie nodded toward the merchandise booth. "Let's go get you some gear."

"You don't need to do that!"

"My son is a Marching Hawk. It's my duty to purchase another shirt. Half the proceeds go to the band."

"When you put it that way, let's go."

They walked over to the stand and Susan picked out a T-shirt. Donnie paid for it and Susan put the orange shirt on over her long-sleeve navy blue shirt. Donnie kissed the crown of her head.

"You even make orange T-shirts look hot," he whispered in her ear. He moved his hand down her side and she shivered.

"Too bad we're surrounded by children," she said.

Donnie straightened up; his eyes were filled with mischievousness. "Maybe after the band performs at halftime, we can sneak off?"

"What did you have in mind?"

"When you were in school, did you ever sneak off and kiss a boy?"

Susan snort laughed. "No, I didn't sneak off, period."

"Let's change that."

"I'm in." Butterflies fluttered in her stomach. The anticipation of sneaking off with Donnie was enticing.

They walked toward the field. The home team bleachers were already at least half full, and according to the scoreboard, kick off wasn't for another twenty minutes. "Thank you for inviting me out tonight. Before we met at the concert, I was really depressed. Getting to know you and spend time with you has helped me to find joy at a hard time in my life."

Donnie wrapped his arm around her shoulders. Behind them, a drum cadence began playing. "That's the band coming out on to the field. Do you mind walking over to the fence? I usually say hi to Sebastian before I go up in the bleachers. This way you can meet him, too."

Susan's chest tightened. She didn't have much experience dating single dads, and she'd never dated a widow, but she was willing to try new things. That was a big part of the relationship she was building with Donnie. He was her wingman, supporting her on her new adventures. Of course, getting up to high school hijinks was a whole different ballgame than meeting a potential partner's teenage child. She regretted not discussing the Haunted Hayride before she'd meet his son. She needed to think about whether that was a deal breaker. He didn't seem to be overbearing or controlling, but she'd been wrong about men before, and she didn't want to find herself in that position again.

The color guard, comprised of many girls and two boys, passed by Donnie and Susan. They all wore navy leotards with lightning bolts of orange, and they carried blue and orange checkered flags. Following them, three drum majors marched in sync, leading the band onto the field.

"What instrument does your son play? I forgot." Susan scanned the marchers to look for Sebastian.

"He plays the trumpet. He's third chair this year."

"That's awesome. Do see him yet?"

A line of sousaphones passed, then the mellophones, and finally Susan saw the trumpets. Donnie shouted, "Go Sebastian!" and waved his arms. Sebastian was taller than most of the other trumpet players.

"Once they are all out on the field, they have a quick meeting. Then the students can come and talk to their parents for a couple minutes before they line up over there." Donnie pointed. "Just past the end zone to get ready for the National Anthem and the player intros. We can go find seats after we say hi."

"That sounds good to me." She wiped her sweaty palms on her jeans. It was cooling off now as the sun was close to setting, but her nerves were causing sweat to run down her back.

"Are you nervous?" Donnie's eyebrows lowered in concern.

"Maybe a little?" she said.

Donnie rubbed her back. "Good, I'm glad I'm not alone."

Susan laughed. "That was not what I expected you to say." She stood on her tiptoes and kissed his cheek right at his beard line. The band was now clustered around a man who looked to be in his thirties. The man was wiry with short dark hair and glasses, wearing a Marching Hawks windbreaker. He was talking animatedly to the band, and then he pointed to an iPad he was holding.

"Is that the band director?" Susan asked.

"Yes, that's Nolan Reeves. This is his first season as marching band director. He started at Marley Creek High last spring."

"Oh, Okay." The band started clapping together and a chant of "Go Hawks" sounded on the field. "Looks like they are heading this way."

Donnie took a deep breath in and out.

Susan shook out her hands. Was she ready for this? No, but it was literally game time. "Let's do this," she whispered.

The boy she'd seen with the dark hair was heading their way. He had a loping walk and covered the field faster than Susan could have run it. He didn't look her way as he reached the fence line. "Hey buddy, how are you doing?" Donnie clapped his son on the shoulder.

"I'm fine," Sebastian mumbled.

"You got that solo tonight, right?"

Sebastian nodded. Susan watched as Donnie pulled on his beard. "Erm, son—"

Sebastian took off his tall cylinder navy-colored hat with an orange plume and a visor and tucked it under his arm. With his other hand, he pushed his long bangs off his face. This was the first time Susan had gotten a good look at him. He had large brown eyes with the long lashes of youth. His nose swooped down to his full lips. She wondered if when he smiled, she'd see Donnie in his face. Susan hadn't seen a picture of Donnie's wife, but she imagined she was looking into her eyes.

"I want to introduce you to Susan. Susan, this is my son Sebastian."

"Bastian. I prefer Bastian."

Donnie rubbed his head. "Right, sorry about that. Bastian, this is Susan."

Susan held out her hand over the fence and Bastian gave her a weak shake. She tried to meet his eyes, but they almost instantly flitted away from hers and over to the sidelines where the cheerleading squad was practicing. "Nice to meet you, Bastian."

"Nice to meet you," he mumbled. He continued to look at the sidelines and the bleachers.

Susan looked at Donnie.

"Right," Donnie said. "Break a leg, Bastian."

"Dad, don't say that. It's only for theater stuff. Just say good luck."

"Good luck!" Donnie said, and Susan chimed in with him. Sebastian ran back to where the band was starting to tune up their instruments.

Donnie sighed. "Sorry about that."

"You don't have to apologize for anything! I think that went as well as it could. I feel relieved. I hope you do, too."

Donnie nodded. "I do feel better. I'm glad that Sebastian, I mean Bastian, knows we're dating. He seemed indifferent and not downright hostile, so that's good, right? I'm sorry, that sounds terrible. I hope you know what I mean."

Susan nodded. "I know, and I think it went okay." Donnie led the way to one of the few empty spots left in the stands. Susan started to sit down, but Donnie stopped her and put the seat cushions on the aluminum bench. "Thank you," Susan said and sat down. "I love how much of a gentleman you are." She scooted closer to him. Now they were touching from knee to shoulder. She leaned her head against him and sighed. "I appreciate the care and attention."

"You know how they talk about 'love languages?'"

Susan nodded. "Total pop psychology nonsense."

Donnie frowned. "I don't know too much about it. I was going to say my love language is taking care of people. I..." he paused. "Like."

Susan felt a pang in her chest. "I'm sorry I was rude. Thank you, that's sweet. I understand what you mean. It makes me feel a little better about what I have to say."

Donnie turned his head. "What's wrong?" His lips were in a straight line.

"Zaina called to thank me for helping with the hayride."

Donnie's face reddened and his eyes flitted away from hers. "Oh, shit."

"What's the deal?"

"I'm sorry, I should have told him I needed to talk to you first. Jasper was asking for help, and it sounded so fun, and it fit perfectly with our high school fun and games. I said we'd volunteer for the fundraiser. They really need a couple to take their place. Are you angry?"

"When were you going to tell me?"

"Honestly, I was so preoccupied with you and Bastian meeting that I completely forgot about the hayride."

Susan nodded. That made sense to her. "I'm not angry, and as long as Brandee can come help with Mom, I'm game for the hayride."

Donnie smiled and squeezed her thigh. She put her hand on his, stilling him. "But you need to know, I don't need or want you to speak for me. It may seem like a pretty small thing. However, it's very important to me. Run things past me. If we are going to continue dating, I need you to understand good communication between us is the most important thing to me." She took his hand in hers. "Please don't ever do that again."

"Got it," he said hoarsely.

Chapter Sixteen

♥

Donnie

Donnie's stomach had finally calmed down. He'd been so stupid telling Jasper they'd volunteer without talking to Susan. They we just starting to date. They weren't old married folks who finished each other's sentences. What an idiot he'd been. He rubbed Susan's back, grateful for her understanding. He'd make sure he didn't sign her up to do anything without talking to her first.

"When does the band come on the field?" Susan asked, looking at the scoreboard. There were forty seconds left in the first half of the game and the Hawks were down by twenty-eight points.

"First the cheerleaders do a routine, and then the visiting team's cheerleaders have their turn."

"Okay," Susan said. A breeze blew their way from the concession stand. The smell of popcorn made Donnie's mouth water.

"That smells good," she said.

"Want me to go get us some popcorn and a drink?"

Susan scrunched up her nose, and Donnie clenched his hand to stop himself from giving her a bop on it, followed up with a kiss. "Do they have hot cocoa?"

"Yep." Donnie stood up. "I'll go get us some."

Susan gave Donnie a kiss on the cheek. He made his way down the bleachers and over to the concession stand. He checked his pocket for cash and watched as the Hawks fumbled the ball. The visiting Fairview Falcons intercepted it and ran it back for a touchdown.

"This game is over," the heavyset blonde man in front of Donnie said.

"My kid is in band. The halftime show is the highlight of the game for me," Donnie replied.

"My daughter is a cheerleader, so unfortunately, I'll be here until the bitter end."

"Good thing you're fueling up," Donnie said.

A few moments later, it was Donnie's turn. He got two of the popcorn and cocoa specials and tipped the Athletic Boosters twenty dollars.

Donnie quickly walked back toward the bleachers. He didn't want to miss any of the marching band performance, and he'd forgotten to ask Susan to take a video if he didn't make it back in time. Just as the band was marching on the field to take their places, Donnie sat down next to Susan. He handed her a Styrofoam cup of hot cocoa and a bag of popcorn. She took it from him, and he kissed her forehead. Then he juggled his food and drink, trying to take out his phone to record the performance.

"Do you need help?" Susan asked.

"I want to record the band; can you hold my cocoa?" Donnie put his small bag of popcorn in his jacket pocket and handed Susan his drink. She held on to them and Donnie got his phone ready to record.

"There he is!" Susan said.

Donnie's heart soared. He was so glad she was cheering on Bastian. If he was going to be in a serious relationship with someone new, they had to be willing to love him too. He knew she had just met his son, but here she was looking for him amongst the sea of Marley Creek Hawks on the football field. The corners of his mouth turned up. He was lucky to have found her. He should write a thank-you note to the Concert Buddy app.

The drum majors mounted their ladders and lifted their batons, one, two, three and the halftime show started. Midway through, Bastian moved to the front of the field. He stood on the fifty-yard line facing the crowd and played his ten-second solo. As soon as it ended. Donnie and Susan yelled "Go Bastian!" in unison. They turned to each other and grinned.

Tears welled up in Donnie's eyes. It had been so long since he'd had someone to share Bastian with. He'd forgotten what it was like to share the pride of seeing his son perform. Of course, she didn't love Bastian yet, but Donnie couldn't help imagining a future where he wasn't just Susan's partner in crime—well, more like partner in reliving some of the foolishness of youth—but also his life partner, as invested in his son as he was.

Donnie shook his head. Was it way too early to think like this? He focused on recording the band's performance and watched the end of the show. The marching band paused as the last notes of their song reverberated over the stands and then everyone clapped. Susan cheered and shouted Bastian's name again and warmth flooded Donnie's veins. She was an amazing woman.

He grabbed her hand as the band walked off the field and the countdown started for the second half. "Let's go see if we can get up to no good."

Susan's eyes lit up, "What did you have in mind?"

"Come with me." Donnie stood up and Susan followed suit. Donnie led the way down the stairs and out of the bleachers.

"Where are we going?" Susan asked as they started crossing the parking lot toward Marley Creek High School.

"You'll see, just trust me."

"Okay," Susan said. "I'm going to go with this. Please tell me we aren't going to get arrested."

"I don't think so," Donnie winked at her.

Susan shook her head and leaned into Donnie. He led Susan along the back of the school until they were at the doors closest to the band room. Donnie paused with his hand on the door.

"They usually keep this door open because after halftime, parents help push some of the percussion equipment back into the school. The students go into the stands to help pump up the crowd by playing parts of songs."

"Like when they play Bah,bah, ah ah ha ha. That song?"

"Right, 'Seven Nation Army' by the White Stripes, all marching bands play it," Donnie said.

Donnie pulled on the door and it opened. He ushered Susan in, allowing himself to grab a handful of her ass as he did. God, she felt good. She giggled and playfully pushed against his chest.

He took her hand and pulled her down the hall.

"Where are we going?" she whispered.

"We are almost there," he whispered back.

They turned a corner, and the school auditorium was in front of them. Donnie pushed open a set of orange doors and started walking down toward the front. The stage was empty, and the room was dark apart from tiny lights lining the aisle and sconces near the stage. Once they were halfway down the aisle, Donnie guided Susan into the row, and they sat down.

"Should I have brought my popcorn?" she joked.

Donnie chuckled. "We've got better things to do with our mouths."

The corners of Susan's lips turned up. She took his face in her hands and kissed him. He leaned into the kiss, tasting the salt from their popcorn earlier. Her tongue darted into his mouth. He pressed into the arm of the chair between them, wanting to get closer to her. She wrapped her arms around his neck as they continued kissing. Her scent enveloped him, and his cock twitched in response as she groaned. He ran his hand up her thigh, wishing she wasn't wearing a pair of jeans. He wanted to feel the silky skin of her thigh against his palm.

Donnie moved away from her mouth and pushed back her hair. She moaned as he kissed the creamy skin under her earlobe.

"Do you like it when I kiss you here?" he asked, licking the spot with his tongue, and she nodded. He sucked lightly on the spot, not enough to leave a mark, but enough that she knew he would if she wanted.

"Do it," she said. "I've never been marked before." Her words lit a fire in him, and he didn't think his dick had ever been this hard. He made sure he was in a spot where her hair would cover his bite and sucked on her tender skin. She took in a sharp intake of breath. He placed his hand over her breast and kneaded it as he finished making his mark. Then he blew air on the heated spot. He delighted in her full-body shiver.

Craving more skin-to-skin contact, he took his hand off her breast and slid it down her side and under her shirt. She kissed him needily as he managed to move her bra to the side. She sighed as his thumb and forefinger rolled her hardened nipple. He had to take his other hand and press against his cock, which was trying to burst out of his jeans. They needed to go somewhere and finish this.

"I need you so bad," she murmured.

He couldn't even find the words to respond.

Suddenly, light flooded the room. Donnie and Susan jumped back from each other as a male voice said, "What's going on in here?"

Donnie extracted his hand from under Susan's shirt. Susan hurriedly fixed her hair and shirt.

The thin man with dark hair walked down the aisle toward them. Donnie realized it was the band director. His ears began to ring. Embarrassment flooded every pour of his being, and his face felt like it was on fire. Susan was pale as a sheet. Donnie's heart fell into his stomach.

"Mr. Larson, is that you?" The band director moved closer to them.

Donnie stood up shielding Susan from view. This was his fault; he'd take responsibility for getting caught. "Hi, Nolan. Sorry about this."

"Frankly, it's been quite some time since I've found a couple of adults in here. I chase kids out of here at least three times a week."

"Do you think we could keep this between ourselves? I'd really hate if Bastian found out." Donnie held his breath.

Nolan pointed back up the aisle. "I'm going back up that way, and out into the hall. A couple minutes from now I'll come back and make sure the theater is empty and lock the doors. Got it?"

Donnie said, "Thanks. I appreciate it."

"For what? I didn't see anything." Nolan winked and then he turned around and started walking to the hallway.

Susan reached for Donnie's hand. "On one hand, I'm mortified. On the other hand, I never got busted by a teacher in high school. Kind of thrilling."

Chapter Seventeen

♥

Susan

After Susan had gotten caught 'necking with a boy,' as her mom would have said back in the day, Brandee had texted to ask if she'd be able to leave by eight. Brandee had gotten a call that her sister's car had broken down and she needed a ride. Donnie and Susan decided between getting caught and Brandee having a family emergency, they should cut their date short.

She'd texted Donnie this morning asking if he'd had to take a cold shower last night, too. Susan also let him know she'd been very happy she had new batteries in her vibrator.

Since yesterday's date had been cut short, Susan was really looking forward to their date on Tuesday. Donnie had invited her over for dinner. Dorothy and Susan were in the kitchen. Dorothy was sitting at the kitchen table. Susan was cutting up butternut squash to make her favorite soup. She wished she didn't have to arrange care for each date. It would be nice to be able to spend the night with Donnie if he asked.

"I don't know if I'm going to like this soup. I like simple things like chicken noodle, minestrone, broccoli cheese," Dorothy said.

"Mom, trust me, this is an award-winning soup. It tastes rich even without any dairy. It's like a spoonful of fall," Susan said.

"Tell me again what's in it?"

"Vegetable stock, two leeks, one potato, one butternut squash. Sometimes I add parsnip to it. Cook until the squash is tender, then puree until it's smooth. If you want to get fancy, and today I do. I'm toasting some of Donnie's sourdough bread and topping the soup with gruyere cheese."

"I don't know about that cheese. I've never had it."

"Trust me, Mom. You like Swiss cheese, right?"

"Yes."

Susan added the chopped butternut squash to the pot on the stove and started rinsing off the large potato. "Gruyere cheese is like Swiss, but better. The best part about this soup is the leftovers taste great. I'll freeze some and we can look forward to having it for lunch on Wednesday after your big morning at the hospital."

Dorothy frowned and fidgeted with her sleeve cuffs. "I hate getting scans. They always have a hard time getting the IV in for the contrast, and it hurts to hold still. Plus, it's cold. They give me a blanket, but it's not enough. I don't know why the doctor insists on this stupid scan."

"Well, if you aren't healing well, then they can't start you on physical therapy, so you can start getting around with a walker instead of that thing." Susan nodded toward Dorothy's wheelchair.

"Suzy, what is the plan for when you must go back to work? How many more weeks of leave do you have?"

"Mom, don't worry about my job. It will all work out. The important thing is getting you back to health."

"The only thing you have going for you is your job. I don't want you to lose it."

Susan ground her teeth. She'd been about to tell her mom what had happened at the university, and then her mom went and insulted her. Heat filled her. Why did her mother have to say things like this? If she had a job to go back to, she'd be working on finding a caregiver right now and heading back home, away from her toxic energy.

"Do you hear yourself? I have plenty going for me, and I could always find another job if I needed to. I have experience and plenty of skills."

"I worry about you. Did something happen with your job? Why are you talking about finding another job?"

Susan took out her aggression on the potato and leeks she was chopping up. She didn't want to explain to her mother that she had in fact, lost her job. She was sure her mother would find a way to say it was her fault. Even though her whole department was slashed. She didn't have the energy to deal with that, or with the fact that her mother was worrying more than usual about finances. As far as Dorothy was concerned, Susan had a job to go back to. She'd just wait until after her mom got some good news at the next doctor's appointment. Then she could tell her about the university. She decided to try changing the subject.

"Donnie wants to cook dinner for me on Tuesday, so Brandee is going to come over for a few hours."

"He's cooking for you? That's a good sign. How old is he?"

"Forty-five, Mom."

"Hmm, he's getting up there. You better make sure he starts taking care of himself. He's a big fellow too."

Susan was back to gritting her teeth and was having regrets about changing the subject. "I don't even know what to say to that. I think I'm offended for him and for me." Susan had her mouth open, ready to reply to whatever caustic remark her mother said next.

"I just don't want you to wind up with someone who might leave you. A-a widow, I mean."

Susan closed her mouth. She hadn't seen that coming. Her mother never alluded to the divorce from her father. She'd always assumed her mother was through with men after they'd divorced. Maybe she'd been wrong, and if that was the case, was that part of the reason her mom pushed people away?

"We've only been dating for a few weeks. You don't have to worry about anything like that."

Susan put the remaining ingredients in the pot, feeling her mother's gaze on her.

"He introduced you to his son, and now he's cooking dinner for you? Seems like you've got a boyfriend."

Susan blushed. "I'm too old for a boyfriend."

"I'm in my seventies. You are barely half my age. What do you kids call it these days?" Dorothy sipped on her ever-present cup of coffee.

"In a relationship? Not seeing other people?"

"It's so much easier to say boyfriend. I think I'll just call him your boyfriend, unless that is a problem."

"No, I don't suppose it is," Susan said.

"What are you going to do about that boyfriend of yours when you go back to work at the university?"

"Why are you still going on about my job?" Susan snapped.

"Fine, fine. You don't want to talk to me. I'll shut up."

***

It was an unseasonably warm afternoon for late October. If it hadn't been for the breeze coming from the North, Donnie would've been sweating. Donnie sipped on his decaf cold brew and reviewed his upcoming special orders.

"Hey, man." A hand clapped Donnie on the back.

"Ethan!"

Ethan plopped down into the chair across from Donnie. His dark hair and beard looked recently trimmed. He was wearing a tight-fitting white T-shirt that showed off his biceps and golden skin.

"You're looking great, buddy!" Donnie said.

"Thanks! I've got about an hour until I have to pick up the twins from their Taekwondo class."

"And you came to hang out with me until then?"

"I did that, and I am dying for one of your big-as-a-dinner plate cookies."

"Technically, they are a couple of inches smaller than a dinner plate. And you are in luck. I have a few cookies left. Your favorite is the toffee chocolate chunk, right?"

"Exactly right."

"Hang tight and I'll go inside and get you one. Did you want something to drink with it?"

"Got any new drinks I can try?"

"I have a maple mocha; you want to try that?"

"Can I get it cold?" Ethan pulled his wallet out and removed a card. He handed the credit card to Donnie, who took it.

"Of course." Donnie closed his binder and got up from the table. "Coming right up." Donnie walked inside his store and went behind the counter to begin making the coffee. His phone buzzed in his back pocket.

It was a text from Susan: a gif of the Swedish Chef from the Muppets. He chuckled and looked for a gif to send back to her. He found one of a chef running around the kitchen furiously and sent that back to her with the caption, *Me, by four a.m. daily!* Donnie shook Ethan's iced maple mocha and poured the drink into a to-go cup. Then he put the giant cookie on a paper plate. Hands full, He walked outside with Ethan's order.

Ethan was scrolling on his phone but put it down when he saw his drink and his giant cookie. Donnie placed both in front of him and then handed back his card with the receipt. "Did you add a tip?"

"Thousand-dollar tip—you know, the usual," Donnie quipped.

Ethan took a long drink of the mocha and then broke off a chunk of his cookie. "Did I die and go to heaven?"

Donnie grinned. "Thanks for the compliment. How's our girl Mable?"

"She's great. They love her over at Ida B. Wells Elementary. Mable has put together a whole new de-escalation protocol, and it's cut crisis team calls in half." Ethan beamed with pride as he talked about his live-in girlfriend.

"That's wonderful. If we can help the little ones with their emotions when they go to junior high and high school, it going to be so much better for them."

"I agree. The district is really investing in helping kids who are struggling, and the teachers too. I guess they are hiring an

Assistant Superintendent of Teaching and Learning this fall to help with that effort."

Donnie's ears perked up. He bet that was something Susan was qualified to do. He knew she'd been out of work since the summer. Maybe he could put in a good word for her. The district superintendent, James O'Brien, stopped in every Wednesday to pick up donuts and pastries for the weekly district staff meeting. He'd even done special orders for his kids' birthday parties.

Donnie wished he had his special-order binder with him. He was almost sure he had the superintendent's cell phone. Donnie could give him a quick call and sing Susan's praises, and maybe then James would reach out to Susan. He smiled, picturing Susan hearing how he'd helped her find a job. She'd throw her arms around him, and maybe even call him her knight in shining armor.

"I bet Mable's mentor, Susan, would be great at that job."

Ethan was stuffing a gigantic piece of cookie in his mouth. He nodded in response. Once he finished his cookie, he said, "Speaking of, Mable said she saw you two out on a date at Jessie's Pub. How's that going?"

Donnie stroked his beard, "Susan is, well, she's amazing and beautiful and kind. She met Bastian at the football game last week."

"Oh wow, so this is serious."

Donnie sat up straighter in his chair. "Yes, it is."

Ethan smiled. "I didn't think I'd ever see you with a woman. You're not a monk anymore."

"Nope, she's coming over Tuesday for dinner."

"I'm proud of you for putting yourself out there, Donnie."

Donnie's ears felt hot. "Thanks, I appreciate you."

Ethan drank the last of his mocha. "I better get going. Time to go pick up the boys."

"We should set up a double date or a game night. What do you think?"

Ethan got up and threw away his trash. "Text me some dates and I'll check with Mable."

"Sounds good!" Donnie walked back into Books and Breads. He pulled his special-order binder out of the drawer and paged through until he found the last order for the district superintendent. His pulse quickened. If Susan found a job in town, she wouldn't have to worry about the costs of taking care of her mom, and she'd be closer to him. How fortunate Ethan had told him about this opening, and the fact that he might be able to help her get the position was icing on the cake.

Chapter Eighteen

♥

Susan

Susan parked her car in Donnie's driveway and checked her watch. She'd promised Brandee she'd be back by ten-thirty at the very latest. It was a school night, and she'd only been able to come over at all because her son was going to be at his dad's for the night. Susan knew even though Brandee was only thirty, she needed her sleep, so she'd be able to chase the preschoolers the next day. She was planning to get back home by ten since Brandee had been gracious enough to come stay with Dorothy for a few hours. Susan rushed up the driveway and the six steep cement steps to Donnie's front door, excited to make every minute until ten p.m. count.

Before caring for Dorothy, Susan wouldn't have given the steps a second thought. But now that she was constantly having to help Dorothy maneuver life in a wheelchair, she was hyperaware of how many places were difficult to navigate. Donnie's stairs didn't even have a railing. What were homebuilders thinking in the eighties? She rang Donnie's doorbell.

The door flew open, and Susan's smile fell from her face.

"Oh, it's you," Bastian said. He flipped his hair out of his face and turned back. "Dad, your friend is here."

Susan stood on the landing, unsure of what to do. Should she just go in?

"Did you let her in? Tell her I'll be right there," Donnie yelled from somewhere in the house.

Bastian turned back to her. "Dad said come in." Then he walked away from the door. Susan stepped into the house. She saw there was a boot tray, and she toed off her shoes and put them next to Donnie's Crocs. Bastian dove over the back of the couch and hit resume on a video game.

Susan's stomach flip-flopped. Was Bastian going to stay in for the night? Had she misunderstood? Had Donnie invited her to a family dinner or an intimate dinner for two? She shifted from side to side, questioning her decision to wear a lacy thong. Donnie walked down the hall wearing an apron and holding a wooden spoon. He enveloped her in a hug.

"I missed you," he murmured in her ear. He gave her a kiss on the cheek. "Come back to the kitchen. Let me get you something to drink." Susan followed Donnie down a short hallway, and to the right, she saw a bedroom with dark blue walls and a bed with a chocolate-colored comforter. The room looked uncluttered, and she assumed it was either a guest room or Donnie's. It didn't have any of the hallmarks of a teenage boy's room.

Across the hall was a powder room with a sunflower theme. The back of the house opened to a large kitchen with a farmhouse theme. Instead of traditional cabinets, there was open shelving. On it was a riot of dishware in various colors.

Susan instantly envied the deep single sink and the stainless-steel counters.

"I'm so jealous of that countertop. Mom's kitchen has tile, and it's impossible to clean the grout."

Donnie smiled, "There used to be tile here, too. I had it taken out about ten years ago when I redid the kitchen." The table was made from a refurbished door and the chairs around the table were mix-matched. Susan was impressed by how the eclectic mix of colors and materials worked to make the kitchen feel cozy and inviting. He pulled out a chair for Susan.

"Would you like a glass of wine?" Donnie pointed to the bottle on the table. "I made veggie lasagna for us, and it should pair well. It's a Sangiovese. I got it from the new wine and cheese shop that opened by Jesse's."

"I'll try it. What's the name of the new shop?"

"Get this, it's called 'A Reisling To Be Happy'," Donnie said. He took his apron off and hung it on a hook by the back door. There were large windows on either side of the door looking out into Donnie's back yard. It was dark out and she wondered what the backyard looked like during the day.

"That's so clever. They'll fit right in with our downtown."

"I agree, the owner wasn't there, but they have a nice variety of wines, and they sell charcuterie boards. The store calls them Adult Lunchables."

"Cute. Sounds like a fun place for a date or girls' night out. Maybe even a book club collaboration?" Susan said.

"That could work. Thanks for the idea."

"Is Bastian staying for dinner or?"

Donnie shook his head. "No. He's going over to a friend's house."

Susan relaxed in her chair. "How are things going with you two? Is he okay with us dating?"

Donnie leaned on the kitchen counter. "As far as I can tell, he doesn't mind. Not like we are talking much. He's still upset I won't let him behind the wheel."

Susan bit her lip. She debated saying something about Donnie's refusal to let Bastian learn to drive. "Of course, it's not my business—"

"Go ahead. What did you have to say?"

"I just think Bastian seems to be a responsible kid and I don't think it would hurt for him to participate in the school's driving program."

Donnie pulled at his beard. She could see a flush on his cheeks. Susan held her breath, hoping she hadn't just blown things with Donnie.

"I appreciate your opinion, but it's my decision and I'm not there."

Susan pressed her lips together. She'd said her peace, and he was right; this wasn't her decision.

Donnie pulled two wine glasses off a shelf and poured each of them a glass. "Back to us."

He held up his glass to toast, and Bastian popped his head into the kitchen.

"I'm leaving now."

"Be safe, I love you," Donnie said back.

Bastian rushed out to meet his friends.

Donnie sighed.

"Teenagers," Susan said.

Donnie nodded. "Now where was I? Right, a toast. To Susan, whose beautiful smile makes my heart sing."

Susan's mouth went dry. She'd never had someone toast to her before, even at her wedding. The toasts were about the happy couple and not her specifically. Joy expanded outward until she could feel it in her toes. "Thank you," she whispered and then she clinked her glass against his. They took sips of their wine and Donnie pulled out her chair.

"Sit down," he said.

Susan smoothed down her short red skirt and sat down in the chair. Donnie hustled around the kitchen, setting the table for two. "Is there anything I can do?"

"No, I've got this. You're my guest. Sit, relax, enjoy your wine."

Susan drank a little more of her wine. Her stomach growled. "The lasagna smells heavenly."

"I haven't made it in ages, so I hope it's as good as I remember."

"I'm sure it will be delicious. I've always found that the food I don't have to cook tastes extra yummy. Are you sure I can't help you?"

"Here," Donnie handed Susan a bamboo bowl filled with salad. She put it on the table. Donnie turned back and pulled the lasagna out of the warm oven. He cut slices and put them on their plates. Susan added some salad and dressing. Her mouth was watering. Donnie waited for her to take the first bite.

She took a bite and smiled. The noodles weren't mushy, and the vegetables tasted very fresh. The cheese had a nice richness to it. She chewed the lasagna and spoke. "Your cooking is as good as your baking. This is amazing."

Donnie beamed. He picked up a remote and turned on jazz music. Susan relaxed further in her chair.

"How are things with your mom? Any news yet?"

"We go first thing tomorrow to get the CT scan done. Then we have to go back the next day for the results. I'm hoping we get good news about how the healing is going."

Donnie stabbed at his salad. He took a bite and chewed. "I can't believe you have to go back the next day for results. What a pain!"

"Tell me about it. I think I spend about twenty hours a week going to and from doctors' appointments with my mom." Susan sipped on her wine and they both finished the last of their lasagna.

"And on Friday, we have the Haunted Hayride. That will be a nice change of pace," Donnie said.

"For sure! The weather looks decent, and my costume is ready. How about yours?"

"All I'm wearing is a pair of jeans and one of my weekend flannels. I get off easy—just throw on a werewolf mask and some furry gloves and I'm ready to go. But now that I think about it, you should have worn your costume." Donnie licked his lips, and his eyes traced Susan's body.

Susan leaned on the table, crossing her arms so that her boobs were pressed up until they were nearly overflowing from her form-fitting red sweater. "Pretend I'm wearing a red cape."

"Should I huff and puff and try to blow your house down?"

"No, silly, that's the three little pigs. You're the big bad wolf. You have big eyes to see me, big ears to hear me, and a big mouth to eat me up!" She jumped up from the table and ran down the hall.

Donnie hopped up and chased her down, picking her up outside the bedroom and carrying her into it.

I was right. This is his bedroom. It smelled like pine and smoke. He deposited her on the bed.

Donnie unbuckled his belt. He pulled out his shirt and unbuttoned it. Susan's mouth went dry. It was finally happening. She couldn't wait to see him completely undressed. Her hand clenched and unclenched, eager to finally wrap her fingers around his cock.

"Take off your sweater, Red."

Susan was happy to oblige. She pulled off her sweater and tossed it to Donnie. He put it on his dresser. Susan licked her lips, moving to the edge of the bed. "Do you have protection handy?"

"Condoms are in the nightstand." Donnie walked over and stood between Susan's legs.

"Fantastic." She looked up at Donnie. He had a dusting of hair on his chest. Her core was throbbing. She could not wait to have him inside her. She wanted to straddle him, but first, she wanted to see and taste his cock. Her lacy red push-up bra was annoying. Each movement she made caused it to scrape against her swollen nipples. She needed more. She wanted Donnie's callused hands on her breasts. Her cheeks flushed.

"God, you're beautiful," Donnie said. A crooked smile was on his face, and he cupped her cheek.

She reached up to the button on his pants. "May I?"

He moved her hand down so she could feel his hard length behind his zipper. "Please."

She held her breath, unbuttoning his pants. She pulled down his zipper and then yanked his pants down. He kicked them off. Underneath, he was wearing silky black boxers. She caressed him through the boxers, taking her time. Then she tried to wrap her hand around his cock, only to find he was too big for her to close her fingers around him. His velvet-soft skin was warm to her touch. She ran her hand over his tip, using a bead of precum to lubricate. Donnie thrust against her hand.

Her pussy was wet in anticipation, but that would have to wait. First, she was going to taste him. Her mouth watered at the thought. Donnie reached over and unclasped the front of her bra. Her nipples burned in the cool bedroom air. He lightly squeezed her breast. His touch was a lightning rod to her throbbing core. She moistened her lips, and gently kissed the tip of his cock. Then she slid her lips around him and took as much of him as she could until he hit the back of her throat. Donnie groaned, and the sound of his need made her bear down. It wasn't going to be long before she was going to have to push him down on the bed and fuck him within an inch of his life.

Chapter Nineteen

♥

Donnie

Donnie ran his hand through Susan's hair and wrapped the brown strands around his hand. "Is this okay?" he asked. The last thing he wanted was to be accidentally rough with her because of his overwhelming need. Instead of giving him a verbal answer, she gave him a thumbs up and continued giving his cock her full attention. "Your mouth looks so pretty wrapped around me."

He lightly pushed her head down. She cupped his balls, and he almost lost it right there. "You are so hot. Susan, I can't take this," he gasped. She sucked his cock harder. He gripped her hair harder, moving her on and off him.

She tapped his hand, and he let go of her hair. She took her mouth off his cock.

"Get the condom," she said, and she laid back on the bed. He watched as she reached down, rubbing her pink clit with her finger. He fucking loved watching her touch herself with her ruby red-tipped fingers. His mouth dropped open and for a moment, he lost his place in time. "Condom," she reminded him.

He pulled open the bedside drawer and took out the condom. He ripped it open and slid it down over his throbbing dick. Once it was on, he knelt on the bed and pulled Susan toward him. He caressed her knees, then pushed them apart, and she wrapped her legs around his waist. Her core lined up against his cock and he took himself in hand and teased her entrance. She moaned, and it sent electricity zipping through his body.

"I don't think I can hold out for long," he said. "You're just too fucking perfect." He slid his length into her wet pussy and groaned when he was sheathed to the hilt inside her. She squirmed against him, and he raised one of her legs over his shoulder so he could adjust his angle inside her. He touched her swollen clit, rubbing his thumb over it. She moaned. "Yes, Donnie, please, fuck me."

That was all he needed to hear. He sped up his pace, turned on by their moans and the sound of their bodies meeting. "You're so tight. I want to stay in you all night."

"Yes, yes, keep fucking me all night. God, you're so big. Yes! Just. Like. That!"

Her words and the way her pussy clenched around him undid him. He came so hard his legs shook. He felt like he must have burst through the condom with the intensity of his climax. Donnie turned his head and kissed her foot as he lowered her leg. Susan wrapped her arms around his neck and pulled him down for a gentle kiss.

"That was worth the wait," she said after they kissed.

Donnie rested his head in the crook of her neck. He kissed her collarbone lightly. "I haven't been this happy in so, so long." He leaned up on his elbow, needing to make eye contact with Susan as he spoke. "I'm falling in love with you, Susan."

Susan bit her bottom lip. "I'm crazy about you, Donnie." Her voice cracked.

Joy bounced around Donnie's chest. She didn't say she was falling in love, but it was close and that would do for now.

Chapter Twenty

♥

Susan

Susan gave the valet her ticket. She hoped they would bring the car around as soon as possible. She wanted to go home, go up to her room, and cry for a little while. Dorothy was quiet for a change, and that just unnerved Susan more. Susan tapped her foot. Where was that valet? It wasn't like the hospital was busy at eleven a.m.

"After this next surgery, I'll just have to go to a rehab facility like they said. You have to go back to work and I can't afford home health."

"Mom, let's talk about this later."

Dorothy worried a tissue in her hand. "I thought I'd be better by now."

Susan's chest ached. As much of a pain in the ass as her mom could be, and even with her judgmental and harsh remarks, she was still her mom. She was in her seventies, probably in pain now, and had just found out she would need to undergo another surgery as soon as possible if she was ever going to have a chance of walking again. Susan gasped as she recalled how her mom used to love going for walks with her girlfriends back in the day.

"Suzy, what's wrong?"

Susan swallowed the lump that had formed in her throat. "Nothing's wrong, I'm fine."

"Okay good. Look, there's the car."

Susan tipped the valet once he'd helped get her mother into the passenger seat. "Wish you could come home and help me get her into the house," she joked.

The valet smiled and thanked her for the tip.

Susan put on the radio, flipping through until she found the nineteen-sixties hits station she knew her mom enjoyed. Dorothy looked out the window as they drove toward Marley Creek. Susan turned on her turn signal and pulled onto the highway.

Now was the time for Susan to tell her mom about her job. Hopefully, at this point, Dorothy would focus more on how this meant Susan could take care of her and she wouldn't have to go to rehab. She'd have to emphasize that she had enough savings to last for a while longer. She was not looking forward to another four to six months of taking care of her mom. But what else could she do? Her mother had no one else.

She cleared her throat. "I have a good news, bad news situation."

"Might as well give me the bad news first. It has been a bad news kind of day," Dorothy said flatly.

"Actually, I don't have a job to go back to. The university closed down my department."

Dorothy gasped. "When did this happen?"

"A few weeks before your accident. Once you fell, I wanted to be here for you, and I didn't want you to worry about my job situation when you needed to focus on healing. Then when you kept harping on about how my job was the only thing, I had going for me, I really didn't want to talk about it. I never thought you'd need another surgery."

"You were going to just leave me once I was back on my feet and not tell me what the university did to you?" Dorothy said quietly.

"That was my plan," Susan said.

"I-I don't understand."

"I didn't want to worry you. I'll be fine. There is still a decent amount of money from the sale of my condo."

"I should be happy that you don't have to leave, but it's really crummy that the university dropped you like a hot sack of potatoes and that you didn't let me into that part of your life."

"I'm sorry," Susan said.

The rest of the drive to Marley Creek passed in silence. Once they exited the highway, Susan spoke. "Would you like to stop at Books and Breads and get coffee? My treat."

Dorothy snorted. "Now that I know you're unemployed, let's hope your boyfriend gives us a discount."

Susan smiled and put on her blinker. She was grateful that there was one open handicap parking spot in front of Books and Bread. If she'd known that Dorothy would be a wheelchair user for months, maybe even years, she would have looked into an accessible vehicle when she came to town. Susan got out of the car and shook her head. She owed it to her mom not to be defeatist. She would be there to help her mother prepare for surgery and then to recover. It would probably be the hardest thing she'd ever done, but she was going to get that stubborn woman back on her feet and walking, even if it took a year or two.

Susan wrangled the wheelchair out of the car and brought it around to the passenger side. She helped her mom get it. At the door, she pressed the automatic door opener. It swung open. The energizing scent of coffee and vanilla wafted over them.

"I think I'd like something to go with my coffee. Suzy, do you want to split a sandwich with me?"

Susan was happy her mom had an appetite after the day she'd had. "I'd love to. You pick the sandwich. I'll try any of them."

Donnie walked out from the book side of the store holding a brightly colored picture book. His eyes lit up as he saw Susan and her mom. "Dorothy, Susan, what a wonderful surprise. You just missed a room full of toddlers and their moms and nannies. I can hear myself think again."

Susan walked over to Donnie, and he gave her a big hug. "That's exactly what I needed," she said.

"Everything okay?" he asked, his eyes filled with concern.

Susan shook her head and whispered, "We just got back from the doctor."

Dorothy perused the menu board. She maneuvered herself up to the bakery case and looked at the cookie and pastry options.

Donnie kissed the crown of Susan's head. "Just let me know if I can do anything to help."

"You're so sweet," Susan said, and she gave him a squeeze before letting go of him.

Donnie walked over to Dorothy. "What can I get you two lovely ladies for lunch today?"

"I'd like a cup of the hazelnut coffee. Black, of course."

"Got it."

"And can I get a turkey avocado sandwich on toasted sourdough?"

"It comes with havarti cheese, arugula, and pickled radishes, too." Donnie said.

"I'll try it with everything. As long as that is okay with you, Suzy?"

"Sounds delish!" Susan said.

"And can you cut it in half?" Dorothy asked.

"Yes. Do you want a bag of chips with it or some fresh fruit?"

"Fruit, please," Dorothy said.

"And can I get an iced chai latte?" Susan asked.

"Coming right up."

"Do you want to sit where we sat last time or at a different table?"

"Let's sit at the same table," Dorothy said.

"It can be our regular table," Susan said. "We can start coming here a couple times a week if you'd like."

"That might be nice," Dorothy said.

Susan pressed her lips together. All things considered, that was as close to a *yes, definitely* as she could expect from her mother. Donnie brought over their drinks and set them down. Then he put a plate with half a sandwich and a small cup of fruit in front of each of them.

"Will you be joining us this time?" Dorothy asked.

Donnie checked his watch. "I've got about ten minutes before I need to start packing lunches for Ida. B. Wells's monthly staff meeting."

"I was wondering how you kept this place afloat. "Whenever we come, we're the only patrons in here," Dorothy said.

Donnie opened and shut his mouth. Susan caught his eye and just shook her head. "That's just Dorothy," she mouthed. Donnie patted Susan's leg under the table. She loved how his touch helped her relax. She imagined what daily life might be like if he was her partner in more than high school adventures.

"I'm lucky Marley Creek supports its small businesses and that we have the train station bringing people from all over."

"I hadn't thought of the commuter traffic. You might be smarter than I gave you credit for."

"Mom!"

A sly grin spread on Dorothy's face. "Suzy, I was kidding. Good gravy, you should know by now when I'm making a joke."

Susan scoffed, "As if you make jokes."

"Maybe I'm turning over a new leaf," Dorothy said.

"An old dog learning new tricks?"

"You wound me, daughter."

Susan looked over at Donnie, who winked at her. "Eat your sandwich, Mom."

Dorothy snorted and then she took a bite of her sandwich. Susan did as well. "This is delicious, Donnie," Susan said.

"Thanks."

"I appreciate you sitting down with us. Mom got some crummy news at the doctor's office and this is a pleasant break."

Donnie's brow lowered. "Is everything okay?"

"I have to have another surgery," Dorothy said.

"Oh no, I'm sorry to hear that."

"My doctor says it's my best chance to walk again." Dorothy took another bite of her sandwich. "And Suzy will be here to help me out, but she needs to find a job."

Donnie looked at Susan, his eyebrows raised. "Maybe I can help?"

Susan put up her hand, "No, I don't want either of you to worry about me. I'll handle it." Susan pointed at her mom. "We need to focus on you being strong for your surgery. Eat some more of your food."

"And you." She pointed at Donnie. "You can focus on just being there for me. I'll worry about my career. Maybe it's time for me to try something new."

Donnie's phone alarm chimed. "I've got to get back to work. If you ladies need any refills on your drinks, just let me know."

Susan leaned over and kissed Donnie on the cheek. Donnie nodded to Dorothy, and he got up and went behind the bakery counter. Susan got a to-go box for her mother and then they left Books and Breads.

Susan was quiet as she went through the rest of her day. She needed to decide her future. Was she going to put down roots in Marley Creek? Or was she going to continue on as a long-term visitor and leave as soon as she could reasonably leave her mother on her own? If she did decide to stay, she needed a job. Was there something available at the community college? What would she do if she couldn't find a job, and where would she live? Could her mom continue to live in this house?

Chapter
Twenty-One

♥

Donnie

Donnie had been too excited about the Haunted Hayride to get in a nap after work. Not only was it helping raise money for the high school, he was going to be spending the evening chasing Susan around. He couldn't wait to see her in that short red skirt that showed off her thick thighs.

He stepped out of the shower and wrapped a towel around his waist. He cleaned off the fogged-up mirror and looked at himself. Lately, he didn't think he looked so bad. Donnie realized he didn't have the urge to suck in his stomach. Instead, he was thinking about how Susan had run her hands over his shoulders and chest, commenting on how strong he was.

He pulled on his boxers, and then his fleece-lined jeans. This was the first time this year he'd had to pull them out, and he was pleased to see they still fit. He put on a long-sleeve T-shirt and his red and black flannel shirt. He looked in the mirror and smiled. The shirt didn't make his complexion look blotchy. Donnie thought he looked nice—maybe even handsome.

He put cardamon and black pepper-scented beard oil on his hands and then smoothed it through his beard and hair. He pulled out his phone and clicked a rock-based Halloween playlist to finish getting ready and get in the mood. Once he finished in the bathroom, he walked out and over to the linen closet, where he kept medicine and bathroom essentials. Just in case Susan or he needed it, he put a handful of cough drops in his pocket. They were going to be giving their vocal cords a rough time since he was going to be howling, and she'd be screaming.

Donnie walked down the half-flight of stairs to where Bastian was playing video games. After he checked his watch, he found he had some time before he needed to leave to pick up Susan. He got a can of seltzer water from the refrigerator, popped it open, and sat down on the couch.

"Did you and your friends decide if you're going to the Haunted Hayride tonight?" Donnie hoped his son wasn't going to be at the hayride. He knew how easily Bastian got embarrassed by him.

"Nah, we're going to go to a haunted house over in Cooper's Hawk."

"Who's driving?"

Bastian kept playing his game and ignored him. Donnie was used to this. He sipped on his drink and waited to see if Bastian was going to crash in the game or level up. Donnie pulled out his phone and checked to see if Susan had texted him. He wondered if James O'Brien had contacted Susan. He'd sounded like he was really interested in Susan's background when they talked.

Donnie thought about what kind of breakfast he would make for Susan on her first day of work. Would she continue to live with her mom? If they continued to date, would she want to move in with him? He let himself dream even further, imagining going to Susan's mom and asking for her hand in marriage. She would be a beautiful bride, and he knew she'd be the best stepmom for Bastian.

"Dad, Dad," Bastian said.

"What's up?"

"I'm getting a ride with one of the drum majors."

"Which one?" Donnie asked.

"Chris. He's a senior. He's going to pick me up."

"Are there going to be other kids in the car?"

"Yeah, but he turned eighteen at the end of September. Plus, he's had his license since he turned sixteen. He's a good driver. He went through the school program. They don't mess around at Marley Creek. That's another reason you should let me do driver's ed!"

Donnie frowned. "I'm not changing my mind."

Bastian threw down his controller. "God, y-you suck!"

Donnie ignored his son's outburst. His son would live waiting longer than some of his peers to get his license. "Keep it up and you'll wait until you are eighteen and get your license that way."

Bastian went back to his video game. "You're the worst," he mumbled under his breath.

"I'm the parent. It's my job to make sure you make it to adulthood."

"You can't control everything," Bastian countered.

"I can try." Donnie said. He pocketed his phone and got up from the couch. "Make sure you are home by eleven. I should be back by then, so don't think you can sneak in late."

"Whatever."

Donnie sighed and put on his jacket. He checked his coat for the keys and then walked out of the house. Parenting a teen was often a slog, but even the argument with Bastian couldn't dampen his spirits. He was on his way to see his girl. Should he ask her to be his girlfriend? Would she think it was sweet if he asked? He hummed "I Put a Spell on You" by Screamin' Jay Hawkins as he started his SUV and drove to pick up Susan.

Chapter Twenty-Two

❤

Susan

Susan and Donnie got out of Donnie's car and started walking toward the park at Marley Lake. Trash cans were placed strategically along the route burning wood. The smoke from the fire filled the air, making it look like a fog was rolling out over the trail. A light breeze rustled the trees and Bluetooth speakers played spooky sounds as they walked closer to the ticket stand.

"We're supposed to check in at the stand and they'll give us some bottled water and make sure we have a walkie-talkie," Donnie said.

Susan nodded. She was wearing tights under her leggings and fur-lined black boots. She'd also put a long-sleeve beige thermal shirt under her dress. Over it, she had her Little Red Riding Hood cape. Now that she was here, she regretted her decision to pass on the faux fur-lined cape. It was chilly, and the temperature was going to drop as the sun finished setting.

Donnie put an arm around her, and she leaned into him. "Are you cold?"

"A little, but I should be okay once we get to our spot. We'll have a fire barrel by us, right?"

Donnie nodded. "Jasper said they put them by all the actors."

Susan paused and looked up at him. "Actors? Oh, I guess that is what we're doing."

"We don't really have any lines, though. You just scream and I growl and chase you."

Susan slapped Donnie's ass. "You better watch it. I might chase you and make you scream."

Donnie waggled his eyebrows. "Bring. It. On. I'm here for it." He pulled her to him and grabbed a handful of her rounded bottom. She leaned into him and kissed his full lips. Susan inhaled his scent and warmth pooled in her abdomen. She wondered if they'd get a break tonight and, if so, could they sneak off into the woods and fool around? That was something she'd never gotten to do in high school.

Donnie kissed the top of her head. He went to speak to someone she didn't recognize who was at the concession counter. Susan wrapped her cape around herself. She pulled her phone out of her skirt pocket and saw she had a new voicemail. It wasn't a familiar number, but since her mom had put her down as an authorized contact for all of her doctors, it could be one of them. She clicked play and held her phone up to her ear.

"Hi, Susan, this is James O'Brien, Superintendent for the Marley Creek School District. Donnie Larson mentioned that you were looking for a job. I took the liberty of looking you up and, based on your background, I'd like to get together with you for a chat regarding an opening we'll have in the new year.

Give me a call when you have a moment and we can schedule something. Looking forward to speaking with you soon!"

Susan's heart began to pound. Heat flooded her body, and she wasn't cold anymore. Here she was standing in a costume about to be part of a Haunted Hayride with a guy who'd volunteered her to be part of the event without checking with her! And now she'd gotten a phone call from a professional educator about a job because that same person had again done something about her without her!

Her heart sank into the ground. They had talked about this! She'd thought he understood she was a grown woman and if they were going to be partners, he needed to ask her before he spoke on her behalf. How dare he try to line up a job interview for her! She wasn't even completely sure she wanted to stay in Marley Creek and she was even less sure that she wanted to stay in education!

Her eyes stung. She was so mad and sad and now she was starting to cry. She blinked back the tears. Donnie would be over here at any minute. She'd been having such a great time, but she couldn't stay with someone who thought it was okay to speak on her behalf! She didn't do this to him. Why was he doing it to her? Especially when it was about her career. He hardly knew anything about her experience and expertise.

If the situation were reversed, she would never speak for him. This was a matter of trust. She needed to be able to trust Donnie and right now, she couldn't do that. She shoved her phone back in her pocket. Not only that, but now she was in an awkward situation. She practically had to meet with James O'Brien, otherwise she would look like a flake. It would make

Donnie look poorly as well. She ought to tell Donnie to call the guy back and explain he overstepped.

Susan looked over at him. He was laughing and collecting a backpack from the concessions stand. Dang it—she'd really thought they might have something that could last. She swallowed her sadness; she'd have to do her best to get through the hayride. There was no way she could leave now. Donnie would look bad. She'd also make Jasper and Zaina look bad as well. This fundraiser gave college scholarships. She didn't even have a way home without him. Unless she called an Uber, did she want to cry in the back of an Uber at her age?

Donnie walked up. The backpack was looped over one of his shoulders. He held out his other hand, and she took it. She didn't speak as they started walking.

"We are the second to last vignette in the Haunted Hayride," he told her. "They added on two extra hayrides this year, so we have six hayrides tonight. There are some cough drops in the bag and bottles of water."

"Okay," Susan said. She wished she was at home in bed. And not her home here in Marley Creek—she wished she was back in her condo and had her old job and her tenure track, but here she was. Her chest was tight. She hated feeling trapped. How ironic she was going to be chased by the big bad wolf over and over again tonight.

They walked on the paved road past a man dressed as a surgeon with fake blood all over his scrubs and a teenager holding fake intestines to his shirt. Donnie and Susan went around a curve. On one side was a giant skeleton head and shoulders that looked like it was coming out of the ground. that,After that they walked past a coffin. It had a motion-activated 'jack in the box' effect, only a vampire popped out of the coffin instead of a clown.

Lastly, they saw a woman dressed in a white nightgown with a ghoulishly white face and long black hair streaked with white. She was standing next to fake headstones. She waved. "Hey, Donnie! Hey, Susan!"

"Hi, Nicole!" Susan said remembering Zaina had mentioned Nicole was also volunteering for the event. Maybe she could give her a ride home tonight instead of Donnie.

"Good luck tonight!." Nicole said.

"Thanks," Donnie said, and Susan mumbled, "I'm going to need it."

"What was that?" Donnie asked as they kept walking toward their designated spot.

"Nothing," Susan said.

"Here we are," Donnie said. In the small clearing a couple of yards away from the trail, where the tractor and trailer filled with hay would go by, there was a large tree stump, and on top of it was a picnic basket. The clearing also had a crackling barrel of fire, and fortunately, the breeze was blowing the smoke away from them.

Susan walked up to the picnic basket and lifted the lid. Inside was an axe. Susan pulled it out and wasn't surprised to find that it was light. She tossed the plastic axe at Donnie. A look of panic flashed across his face, followed by relief.

"Of course, the axe is fake," he said, shaking his head. He tossed it from hand to hand and then he set it down on top of the picnic basket. "Want to come over here, and I can warm you up?" he asked, opening his arms.

"I'm good," she said flatly. The heat of her anger was keeping her quite warm now. She cleared her throat. There was no way she was going to make it through the night without saying something. When she tried to swallow, words stuck in her throat.

"Is something wrong?" He frowned and his eyebrows furrowed. The sun had set. The light from the fire flicked across his face, making him look like he could be the big bad wolf.

Susan's heart clenched. She should be hot and bothered with lust for him right now, but instead, she wanted to cry and punch him at the same time. She gritted her teeth.

The walkie-talkie on Donnie's belt chirped. And a voice said, "First hayride is on the trail."

She had to suck it up and wait until after the hayride to confront Donnie. Her stomach roiled. She stomped her feet to get out some of her frustration.

"So now we just wait for the tractor driver to radio us when they leave Nicole's station, then we have about a minute. We'll see the tractor headlights and get ready to start our little skit. How do you want to play this?"

"Thanks for asking my opinion and not deciding for me," she bit out.

Donnie moved closer to her. "You seem upset."

"Now's not the time to talk."

Donnie nodded his head. "Okay. Fine."

"Fine," Susan echoed. Donnie gave her a puzzled look but didn't say anything. Susan pulled her cape closer around her. Her anger had cooled for now and the wind had picked up. She moved closer to the fire.

"Ah, how did you want to do this?" Donnie asked.

Susan looked back at Donnie. Her chest ached with unshed tears. She'd been looking forward to being campy and silly tonight and, most of all, having fun with Donnie. *So much for that.* "I guess the easiest would be for me to be walking along here and you pop out of the bushes there and start chasing me."

Donnie nodded his head. "Sure, we can do that. I'll growl and then you scream?"

"Works for me."

The walkie-talkie cackled, and a man's voice spoke, "Leaving Resurrection Mary."

"We're up next," Donnie said. He stood to give Susan a hug. She let him but didn't hug him back. This time, he didn't kiss the crown of her head. She wondered what he thought she was upset about. Susan didn't like that she couldn't clear the air and get on with her life, and she didn't like how cold it was even though she had on layers of clothes. She should have brought a jacket to wear between hayrides.

The headlights of the tractor moved through the trees. Butterflies filled her stomach. She hadn't performed in front of an audience in ages, but this was a fundraiser. She was sure the guests were there to have a good time and weren't going to rate her acting skills.

Donnie jumped out of the bushes, and she screamed. She'd been so distracted she'd forgotten he was going to do that. Her flight mechanism kicked in and she ran from him. He chased her in a circle and then she ran behind the flat bed where the guests were sitting on hay bales.

"Help me! The big bad wolf is after me!"

"I'm hungry, little girl! Come back here!" Donnie yelled. The hayride went around another curve and Donnie and Susan hung back. They were quiet as they walked back to their area.

Donnie reached into his pocket. "Want a throat lozenge?"

"Sure," Susan said.

"Do you want to talk now?" Donnie asked.

"How much time do we have before the next group?"

Donnie looked at his watch, before he could answer, the walkie-talkie chirped, "Round Two on the trail."

"Ten minutes, I guess."

"Let's just focus on what we are here to do, and we can talk when it's over."

"Is everything okay? Did something happen to your mom or something?"

Susan's heart ached. "My mom is fine. Well, I mean, nothing has changed there."

Donnie went quiet. They didn't talk while they waited for the next group. Then they did their little skit and went back to being quiet.

Susan was ready to pull out her hair by the time the last hayride drove through. As they trudged back to their spot after chasing the last hayride, Susan let her frustration and words bubble up.

"Did you need to tell me anything?" she asked looking sideways at Donnie.

"Thanks for doing this with me tonight?" he said.

"Remember what we talked about at the football game?"

Donnie looked at her. She could tell he was trying to figure out where their conversation was going. "Do you mean about not signing you up for stuff?"

"I asked you not to speak for me!"

"And I haven't!" Donnie picked up the plastic axe and put it in the picnic basket.

Susan pulled out her phone and waved it at Donnie. "Then why did I get a message from the school district superintendent wanting to do an informal interview next week?"

Donnie's face brightened. "James O'Brien called you? That's great!"

Susan crossed her arms. "Did I ever say I was looking for help finding a job? Did I ever ask you to see if you knew anyone who was hiring?"

"No, but—"

"Exactly. I didn't, and yet you went ahead and decided what I wanted! I don't need you to line up job interviews for me! And it's not even really about the specific situation you've put me in, it's that you didn't even bother to ask me what I wanted! It's so patronizing!"

Donnie dropped his head. "I'm sorry."

"I trusted you. I thought after we talked about respecting me enough not to speak on my behalf that you understood. But I was very wrong."

Even in the low light of the fire, she could see Donnie's ashen face. Her heart was breaking for both of them.

"I just wanted you and your mom not to be stressed out. So I called the superintendent, and he was really excited to hear you were looking for a job."

Susan groaned. "Oh, my God. I can't do this. I don't need you making decisions for me. I'm a grown woman, I've been speaking for myself for decades. Who asked you to do this?"

"I was just trying to help," Donnie said quietly.

"If you were just trying to help, why didn't you ask me beforehand?"

"I thought it would be a nice surprise. I wanted to make things easier for you. I didn't know you'd be upset. I thought I was doing you a favor."

Susan laughed bitterly. "You thought wrong, and I guess I thought wrong as well! I thought you were kind and considerate, and that you appreciated open communication as much as I did. I thought we could work together. I let myself think we might build a life together. A life based on lots of love, crazy good sex, and most of all, mutual respect! But I was wrong!"

Donnie put his hand on her arm. "Susan, please. Listen, I made a mistake."

Susan shook off his hand and turned away from him. "I'll find my own way home." She said and she ran toward the trail. Once she was on the path, she texted Nicole.

> SUSAN: Are you still at the hayride? I need a ride home.

> NICOLE: I'm turning in my stuff at the concession stand. What's wrong? Are you okay?

> SUSAN: No, I'm not okay. I broke up with Donnie.

> NICOLE: Oh no! I'll wait for you here.

> SUSAN: Thanks, I'm almost there.

Susan pocketed her phone and even though her feet were killing her, she picked up her pace until she was jogging. The last thing she needed right now was to run into Donnie at the concession stand.

Nicole saw her and ran over to her, giving her a big hug. "I'm so sorry."

"Can we get out of here? I really don't want to see him anymore tonight." Susan's teeth were chattering. She didn't know how much of it was from the cold and how much was because of the emotional shock.

Nicole put her arm around Susan's shoulders, and they walked to her car. She had started it as they walked so it was warmed up when they got inside. "Do you want to talk here, or should I start driving to your house?"

"Let's start driving, I just want to get away from here," Susan said.

"On it," Nicole said.

Susan sniffed. Tears flowed down her cheeks, and she hated to think how awful she probably looked considering how much makeup she'd put on for their performance tonight.

Nicole opened the center console and took out a packet of tissues. "Here, take as many as you need."

Susan took the packet and pulled one out. Going from the cold outside to the dry warm air of the car was making her nose run almost as hard as she was crying. Susan blew her nose. "Turn left here," she pointed.

Nicole turned and drove past Ida B. Wells Elementary.

"At the next light, make a right. Then our house is the white Cape Cod, about halfway down the block."

"Oh, you don't live that far from me," Nicole said.

"Nuh-uh," Susan mumbled, pulling another tissue from the packet and wiping her nose. The car was quiet, and a phone buzzed. Susan's pocket was vibrating. A lump formed in her throat. She just knew it was Donnie. She didn't want to check the display, but on the off chance it was her mom or Brandee calling, she needed to answer it. Donnie's face lit up her screen. She clicked the refuse button and put the phone back in her pocket.

Nicole's blinker clicked as she slowed down and turned onto Susan's street. Nicole pulled up in front of the house. Susan's phone chimed. She had a new message. She stared at her phone, unsure if she could stand to hear Donnie's voice right now.

Nicole looked at the time on her dashboard, it was ten-fifteen. "I've got time to talk—or I mean, I have time to listen, if you want to talk about it," Nicole said.

Susan dried her eyes again. "Thank you. I just need to let Brandee know I'm out front so she can leave."

Nicole put the car in park and patted Susan's shoulder. "I'm so glad that Brandee is working out for you and your mom."

"She is the best," Susan said, her mood lightening a little. "My mom can be so cantankerous but she's sweeter to Brandee than she is to anyone, including me." Susan texted Brandee, then she took a deep breath and listened to the voicemail.

"Please let me know that you made it home safely. I won't be able to sleep without knowing. Please. I'm so sorry I upset you."

Susan ground her teeth. She would go ahead and send him a text letting him know she was home, but that was it. He hadn't even said he was sorry for what he did. He must not understand what this was really all about. If he couldn't understand why she was ending their relationship, there wasn't anything else she could say to him.

She quickly texted Donnie that she was home. She put away her phone. In the driveway, Brandee got in her car and backed out. As her brake lights faded away, Susan turned to Nicole and explained why she'd broken up with Donnie. Nicole was an excellent listener as Susan poured out her disappointment and sadness.

"I'm so sorry, hon," Nicole said patting Susan's hand.

Susan blew her nose again. "If I catch a cold from the stress right now, I'll be so pissed."

"Get those zinc tablets they sell at the drugstore. I swear by those and I'm constantly surrounded by germy kids."

"True, you would know about avoiding colds," Susan said.

Nicole nodded.

"I don't know what I'm going to do now. I'm really stuck. Thanks to Donnie I'm going to have to meet with the superintendent even though I'm not looking to go back into education." Susan surprised herself with the conviction in her voice. She was done with education; it was time for her to move on.

"I wish I knew the superintendent better. All I know is that he drops off the leftovers from his staff meetings in our teacher's lounge and it's aways yummy food. I only see him a few times a year. "

"I hate that Donnie put me in this situation. I'm so angry with him! But at the same time, I can't throw him under the bus and say that Donnie contacted him without asking me."

"I get it. It really stinks. I was really rooting for you two. Donnie seems so considerate. I'm surprised this happened."

"Maybe I'm overreacting. Maybe his heart was in the right place. I know I have a really strong independent streak." Susan brushed her hair back from her face. "I didn't need a degree in psychology to understand that growing up with my mom who didn't have much use for men or romantic relationships played a part in it."

"This just stinks," Nicole said.

Susan looked at the clock on the dashboard. It was after eleven p.m. "I'm sorry I've kept you so long. You need to get home to your hubby."

"He'll be fine. Take as long as you need," Nicole said.

"You are so sweet."

"That's what friends are for. You are part of our little group now. Zaina and Devin would do the same, and I know you'll be there for us in the future."

Susan teared up again, but this time it wasn't about Donnie. It was about her new friendships. She'd only been back in Marley Creek for a couple of months, but she'd forged some strong relationships. She sniffed and brushed the tears from her eyes, and leaned across the seat to give Nicole a hug.

"This means so much to me. Thank you. I think I'll be okay for tonight at least."

"If it's okay with you, I'll add you to the group chat?"

Susan nodded. "I would like that."

Susan got out of the car and walked to her front door. Once she locked the door and went inside, Nicole drove off.

The house was dark and quiet, aside from the snores of her mother in the living room. Susan took off her shoes and tiptoed up the stairs. She quickly changed out of her clothes, considered throwing her Little Red Riding Hood outfit in the trash, and then took off the remainder of her makeup. She avoided looking at herself in the mirror and tried not to think about Donnie. Tomorrow she'd call the superintendent.

Chapter

Twenty-Three

♥

Donnie

Donnie rolled over and stared at his alarm clock. It was now ten minutes past two. Ten minutes since he'd last looked at the clock. He should give up trying to sleep at this point. It wasn't going to happen, and he had to get up by three to get ready and go to the bakery, anyway. His stomach roiled. He was nauseous and his throat was sore. His head ached from the lack of sleep and the cold air earlier—and probably the fire, too. But he knew if Susan hadn't broken up with him, none of that would matter, and he'd have slept like a rock.

Maybe it was better this way. He could go back to focusing on his business and his son. He needed to make sure Bastian was gearing up for junior year. That was going to be crucial to his college career. His love life was secondary to making sure his only child got into an excellent college. He should have stuck to his original plan of not dating until Bastian had left for school.

Donnie rolled over flat on his stomach, and he inhaled a whiff of Susan from the pillow. He'd changed the sheets after she'd been over, but he hadn't changed her pillowcase. His chest tightened. It was over; she was never going to be in his bed again. He rubbed his chest, trying to relieve the ache. He kept his face in the pillow for a few minutes, almost drifting off to sleep, and then he jolted fully awake. Was he repeating old habits? He got up and dragged himself to work.

Donnie sleepwalked through work, even though he'd been mainlining espresso all day. He took out a couple of antacids and chewed them up. His stomach was a mess and every bone in his body ached. Could being brokenhearted manifest as the flu? He checked his watch and saw that it wasn't even ten a.m. Donnie rubbed his eyes. Thank goodness Tot Story Time wasn't until tomorrow. He didn't think he could handle a room full of two-year-olds today.

Donnie pulled out his phone and saw a text from Jasper.

JASPER: You need to talk?

DONNIE: Bad news travels fast?

JASPER: Looks that way. Maybe talking can help?

DONNIE: I'll come over after Bastian gets here.

JASPER: First drink is on me.

DONNIE: Great, a beer to cry in.

> JASPER: I take that back. My beer is too good to cry in. You can have a water if you want to do that.

> DONNIE: See you this afternoon.

The rest of the morning trickled by. Donnie was consumed by thoughts of Susan and how she'd dumped him. He felt frozen, unable to think, and a weight was on his chest pushing him down.

Donnie stared at the FedEx shipment. He needed to unpack the boxes and set up the display of new releases for November. Donnie pulled out his X-Acto knife and sighed. He always looked forward to the Christmas cozy mysteries and romances. But now, he couldn't stomach any of it. Even the punny titles were setting him on edge: *Candy Cane Slain*, *All I Want for Christmas is A Boyfriend*, *Gun Gun Rudolph*, and *Silent Knight, Hottie Knight*. Normally, he'd be laughing and groaning at the titles and book descriptions. Today he might as well be reading his Excel expense spreadsheet for all the joy this was giving him. Donnie went through the motions, checking his packing slip against the order he received.

***

Donnie sat down at the bar. He caught his reflection in the mirror behind the bar and quickly averted his eyes. He looked like he'd been on a three-day bender. His eyes were bloodshot, and he had dark circles under his eyes. His hair was more disheveled than tousled, and his cheeks were ruddy, the way they got when he didn't sleep well. This is why he tried not to look in mirrors. He'd forgotten himself for a while. His neck heated as he thought about the other day and how he was preening in the mirror before going to the Haunted Hayride. That was supposed to be a fun night, but it had turned into his own personal horror show.

Jasper walked out of his office and over to Donnie. He sat down on the stool next to him. "You look like shit, man."

Donnie's head dropped. His eyes stung as they teared up again. He pressed his thumb and forefinger to the bridge of his nose, trying to stop the sting. He cleared his throat. "I feel like shit, too."

Jasper rubbed Donnie's shoulder. "I get it. I've been there." Jasper motioned to Jax who was behind the bar. They nodded and moments later, Jax set down a beer in front of Donnie and Jasper.

Jax patted Donnie's hand and Donnie took their hand in his. "Thanks, Jax."

Jax tossed their long black hair with red highlights. "Anything I can do to help?"

"I guess I just need someone to talk to."

"You've got me and Jax. What happened?" Jasper said.

Donnie told Jasper and Jax all about how things had been going with Susan and what had happened at the hayride. Jax had to pop in and out of listening mode because they needed to get drink orders for people at the bar and those who came up to the carry-out window for refills on growlers and six-pack pickups. Donnie's throat ached as he tried to speak without crying. The last thing he wanted to do at this point was break down in front of Jasper's regulars and several familiar faces from Books and Breads.

When Donnie was done, Jax brought him over a second pint of beer. Donnie waved it off. "I can't drink that. I'll fall asleep right here and then I'll toss and turn when I should sleep tonight."

"No worries—it's our non-alcoholic pale ale."

Donnie raised an eyebrow. "It is?" He took a few big gulps. "Dude, that is tasty. Thanks for that."

Jax nodded and went down to the window to help a customer.

Donnie looked at Jasper. He could tell Jasper had things to say to him. Donnie thought that Jasper's warm brown eyes were filled with pity for him. He was sure Jasper didn't have problems like his. Jasper came from money, had a distribution deal for his craft beer across the nation, and everyone knew about his whirlwind viral romance with Zaina. All that was on top of his chiseled chin and long, lean runner's body.

"Very few people know this, but after hearing about why Susan ended things, I think I need to share what happened when Zaina and I were dating. Maybe it will give you some hope or some food for thought."

"Please, I'm desperate for a scrap of hope." Donnie said. He fidgeted with the coaster on the bar.

Jasper continued, "Back then, I didn't realize she had no trust in me. So much so that Zain set up a test for me. Well, I didn't know I was being tested, and it led to an embarrassing meeting between me and my now father-in-law. All of it could have been avoided if she hadn't been trying to manipulate people to get her desired outcome. Which she didn't get! All it led to was

Zaina and I splitting up. It also changed her formerly wonderful relationship with her stepdad. It's better now, but I don't think it will ever be what it once was."

"So, what you're saying is I really messed up and Susan was right to tell me to shove off."

"Partly, and also, I'm trying to say maybe all is not lost."

"I guess, but I don't think what I did was so wrong. I didn't trick anyone. I just made a call to a business connection and told him Susan could be a great candidate for a job. Most people would be thrilled."

Jasper frowned. "Susan clearly wasn't."

"I was thinking of waiting a few days, so she could cool off and then maybe give her a call. What do you think?" Donnie said as he knocked on the bar to release some of his nervous energy.

"Man, I don't know. She's made it pretty clear she doesn't appreciate you deciding things for her. Wouldn't reaching out to her just be more of that?"

"You really think so?"

Jasper ran a hand through his shoulder-length black hair. "I'd say, give her some space and try to think about things from her point of view."

Donnie shrugged. "I guess you are right. I just don't understand why it's a bad thing to try to help someone you are crazy about. I wanted to make her life easier."

"But did she ask you to help?"

"No, but I think she shouldn't have to." Donnie's blood heated up as he tried to explain his position. He knew Jasper was trying to help him, but he couldn't stop feeling defensive. Maggie flashed in his mind. He'd worked very hard to avoid dwelling on the events of the day she'd lost her life in the car crash. But sometimes in times of stress, those memories surfaced. He was tired and sad, and he couldn't deal with more regrets right now, so he told his brain to stop digging into the past.

Jasper gave him a half smile. "Just think about what I said, and remember, whatever happens, I'm here for you. Will I see you at the Turkey Bowl?"

Donnie shook his head, "I don't think so. Bastian will be performing with the band, but I rarely go. I didn't go to Marley Creek High, so the annual reunion football game doesn't hit the same for me."

"I always forget you didn't move here until you were in your twenties," Jasper said.

"I'll think about you while I'm at home on my couch."

Jasper laughed. "If you change your mind, come out. It's always a fun night, the big kickoff to Thanksgiving week."

Chapter Twenty-Four

♥

Susan

Saturday afternoon was unseasonably warm, but Susan was too miserable to enjoy the day. Her stomach was queasy, and she wished it was from the stomach flu instead of a broken heart. She saw the cloudless sky and the last of the golden leaves clinging to the maple tree that had been a seedling when she'd last lived at home, but it didn't warm her heart like it usually did.

Susan sat on the back porch with Dorothy and tried to read a book. After re-reading the same paragraph several times, she gave up. It was no use. All she could see was Donnie, and all she could think about right now was him, and it just made her mad. She considered texting the group chat. She needed a distraction from thinking about Donnie and how safe she felt in his arms. True, she loved that he made her feel cherished, but that didn't mean she wanted him to dictate her future.

She put down her book and sighed.

"What's wrong, Suzy-Q?"

A ghost of a smile passed over Susan's face. "You haven't called me that since I was a kid."

Dorothy touched her hand to her heart. "You'll always be my little Suzy-Q in here."

Maybe it was the emotional exhaustion of the last twenty-four hours, but Susan's eyes began to tear. Before she could stop herself, tears were rolling down her face.

Dorothy moved her wheelchair over to Susan. She leaned over and wrapped her arms around Susan. Dorothy smelled of Noxema and Ivory soap, just like she had when Susan was a kid. "It's okay, Suzy, let it out."

Susan allowed herself to cry in her mother's arms in a way she hadn't since she'd fallen off her bike as a kid. When her sobbing stopped, she sat back in her chair.

"Do you walk to talk about it?" her mother asked.

Susan nodded as she realized she did want to talk about it. Forty-five minutes later, Dorothy was up to speed on what happened.

"Do you want any advice or did you just need someone to listen?"

Susan breathed in sharply. She couldn't recall any time in her life when her mother had held her tongue and not given her very strong opinions and advice. She was hesitant, but she had to know what her mom's thoughts on her breakup were. "I'll listen to your advice, but I'm not sure I'll take it."

Dorothy pursed her lips. "That's fair."

Susan couldn't hold her tongue any longer. "Who are you, and what have you done with my mother?"

Dorothy smiled. "It's me. I'm here. I've had a lot of time to think lately, and I'm realizing I don't control even half of what I thought I did. Maybe it's time for me to let that shit go and accept myself and other people as they are. I tried to control you and see how that turned out. The minute you could move out you did, and you didn't come back until now. Let's face it, that was the only upside to this." She gestured to her hip. "Now that I've heard what happened between you and Donnie. I realize that's my fault, too."

"How so?" Susan asked.

"How many times over the years did I tell you that you couldn't do something?"

"Hundreds of times? Maybe more?"

"And how often did I talk about how I didn't need a man telling me what to do?"

"Every day."

"I know I don't have a college degree, but it seems to me that the way I raised you didn't set you up to have an easy time falling in love or giving someone a second chance."

Susan held on to the last part of her mom's words. "You think I should try to get back together with Donnie?"

"You're the only one who can decide that. I will say I think he is kind, and kindness is hard to find in this world. If I could go back in time, I think I'd try to make time to find someone kind to share life with. Being alone is a long road." Dorothy fidgeted with the buttons on her cardigan as she talked.

Susan recognized her mother's nervous search for a cigarette. Watching her looking so small and forlorn, she was struck with the realization that her mother had never shared her feelings with her before.

"Mom, I'm not sure what I'm going to do about Donnie, but I think I know what I want to do when I grow up."

Dorothy's eyebrows knit together. "What do you mean by that?"

"I'm going to tell the superintendent I'm not interested in the job," Susan said.

"I figured you wanted to go back to a university," Dorothy said. "We can work that out so you don't have to stay here any longer." Her tone was flat.

"No, no, Mom, not that either."

"Oh? What's your plan, then?"

"I want to open a community center for the elderly."

"You might want to work on the name. I don't usually speak for all people around my age, but I will say we don't like being called elderly."

"Duly noted!" Susan grinned.

Chapter
Twenty-Five

♥

Donnie

Donnie put his sourdough starter on the counter. The glass jar he used was looking crusty, so he was planning to put his starter in a temporary plastic container and run it through the dishwasher.

The ovens were filled with dozens of muffins for a large breakfast catering order he had in the morning. Thankfully, muffins kept well when they were made ahead of time, unlike some other pastries. The local Lutheran church was having its annual fall gathering, and this was the second year Donnie was contracted to supply twelve dozen muffins. Donnie breathed in the comforting scent of walnuts, cardamon, and cinnamon.

Today could be the day he got up the nerve to contact Susan. He sighed and went back to cleaning off the stainless-steel counter. It had been over a week since the awful hayride. He should leave things alone. Like Jasper had pointed out, Susan didn't want to hear from him. Donnie tossed his rag into his laundry bin and checked the time on his smartwatch. Once again, it was after three-thirty, and Bastian was late. Donnie wasn't in the mood to deal with texting, so he called his son. He put the phone on speaker and readied himself to try not to yell at his son for being late again.

The phone rang once and went to voicemail. "Bastian's busy right now. Text me, 'cause I'm never going to listen to this voicemail." Donnie gritted his teeth and hung up the phone. Now he was pissed. All he asked was for his son to be on time to help out at the business that had helped clothe and feed him for his entire life, and the kid couldn't be bothered to do it.

Lucky for Bastian, Donnie didn't have time to dwell on his son's lateness. The timer dinged, and it was time to take out the muffins. He pulled each of the trays and carefully turned them over onto the waiting cooling racks. Once that was done, he took off his apron and sat down in his cafe with a glass of water.

He rubbed his knee. With each minute that passed, he got more frustrated with his son's attitude. The disrespect. He was going to have to have a serious talk with his son, maybe even ground him. His face flushed. He hated this. His phone rang. Donnie opened it without paying attention to who might be calling him.

"Bastian, where are you?"

"Hey, buddy, this is Jasper. I'm in the parking lot of the hardware store."

"What's going on? Why are you calling me from the parking lot?"

"There's been an accident."

Donnie broke out in a cold sweat. His stomach roiled, and he felt lightheaded. "This can't be happening again! What happened?!"

Donnie got up and started pacing the room. He was going to throw up.

"Bastian is fine!" Jasper said.

Donnie was flooded with relief. The excess adrenaline made him shaky. "Oh, thank God." Donnie burst into tears.

"Donnie, Bastian is fine, but he hit my car."

"You mean he was in the car that hit your car? He doesn't have a license, so, oh my, did you hit your head?"

"Donnie, you better come over here. I didn't hit my head. Bastian was driving, and he rear-ended my car."

Donnie could barely hear Jasper through the blood rushing to his head. He couldn't wrap his mind around the fact that his son had not only defied him, but he'd broken the law and hit a car! Donnie put the closed sign on the door and drove over to the hardware store.

Jasper was leaning against his sapphire car. In front of his car, was an old Toyota Corolla. Three boys stood around that car on their cell phones. Donnie's shoulders dropped in relief. He was so glad to lay eyes on his son and see that he was fine. Grounded for life, but physically fine. Donnie pulled up next to Jasper and parked his car.

He took some deep breaths to try to calm down before getting out of the car. He really wished that Susan was here with him. Over the years, there had been so many times when he'd wished Maggie had been there next to him for support. This was the first time he'd thought of Susan that way. Too bad it was too late, and she'd dumped him. With that mix of emotions, Donnie greeted Jasper.

"Man, I'm sorry this happened," said Donnie.

"Kid's damn lucky it was me and that I was alone. If Zaina was in the car with me, I wouldn't be so chill."

Donnie's blood pressure went back up. This could have been the start of a nightmare. "Are you going to file a police report?"

Jasper crossed his arms. "You don't even have to ask that, especially now that I know your son doesn't have his license. I don't want one dumb mistake to derail his life. You just better make sure he doesn't do anything like this again."

Donnie let out the breath he'd be holding. "Thank you."

"It's not your fault," Jasper said.

Donnie walked around to the back of Jasper's car and looked for damage. "Let me know how much it's going to cost to get your car fixed."

"Donnie, I don't want you to have to pay for it to be fixed."

"Trust me, it's not me that's going to be paying. It's coming out of Bastian's pay."

Jasper nodded, "That's fair. I'll take it and have it looked at and let you know. Since you're here now, I'm going to take off. I'll text you later."

"Sounds good, thanks again, Jasp."

Jasper got in his car and Donnie walked over to talk to his son. Bastian was slumped against the Toyota with his arms crossed.

"Bastian, get in my car." He nodded at the two other boys. "Whose car is this?" A tall boy with an afro raised his hand. "It's mine." Donnie was sure he'd seen this kid with his son before, but he didn't remember his name. "What's your name?"

"Eddie."

"Okay, Eddie, I'm not going to ask you why Bastian was driving your car. That's something I'll take up with him. Please know that we all got off lucky today. Jasper is a friend of mine and he isn't going to report your car hitting his to the police or his insurance company. This could have been so much worse. Since it was your car, you could be held liable for the accident. Do you understand that?"

"I do now, sir," Eddie said, keeping his eyes on the ground.

Donnie walked around the car, "Eddie, was the bumper dented here before the accident?"

Eddie walked over and looked at where Donnie was pointing. "I'm pretty sure it was, but it's hard to tell. This car is super old. My brother and my sister drove it when they were in high school."

"Gotcha, that's actually great news. So, no need to fix anything on your car."

"Nope."

"And you'll never let someone without a license drive your car again."

"No, sir."

"Great talk, Eddie."

Donnie walked away from Eddie. He clenched his jaw. What in the world had his son been thinking? If anyone should understand the dangers of a car, it should be Bastian. Donnie shook his head. He opened the car door and got it. Bastian was on his phone.

"Put your phone away. We need to talk."

Donnie put the car into gear and drove toward home. He should go back to work. But he needed to deal with his son first. The business would have to wait until the morning. Bastian lifted his head from the bent angle it was at to stare as they drove past Books and Breads.

"Wait, we aren't going to the shop? Don't you have to go back to work?"

"Both of us should be there today. But some things are more important than work. I'm not going to ignore what you did for even a few hours. We're going home and getting to the bottom of this. I raised you better than this."

"If you'd just let me take the driving class…" Bastian mumbled.

"I know you aren't talking back right now when I've had to ask my friend not to report you to the police."

"Whatever," Bastian said as Donnie gripped the steering wheel and ground his teeth.

Donnie put on his turn signal and waited for the traffic to clear. "If you ever want a driver's license, you should get your head out of your phone and pay attention to what is happening when I'm driving. Get a feel for how traffic flows and when it's safe to turn."

Bastian didn't respond, but he put down his phone and looked out the window.

Donnie took that as a sign he was actually listening, and he kept driving. Two minutes later, Donnie pulled into the driveway and turned off the car. Before he could say anything, his son had jumped out of the car and gone into the house.

Donnie slowly walked up the stairs and into the house. He felt unsteady on his feet. The shock of Bastian's near miss was still reverberating. He hung up his coat and took off his shoes. Bastian wasn't on the couch playing a video game or standing in front of the open refrigerator, letting all the cold air out. Hopefully, that meant he understood how serious this was.

Donnie peeked into Bastian's room. He was on his bed, headphones on, eyes shut. This was as close to a perfect time to talk as he could hope for. He sat down on his son's bed. The twin bed creaked under his weight. Donnie shifted nervously.

"Do you have any idea what you put me through?" Donnie blurted. He winced. This wasn't how he wanted this conversation to go. He was tired of being at odds with his son.

"I screwed up! Yes, it was a dumb idea to drive Eddie's car, but to be fair, it's kind of your fault. You don't let me do things everyone else gets to do, and I just got sick of it. I'm never allowed to sleep over at a friend's! You only let me do stuff if it's part of the band, and you won't let me learn to drive! Plus, on the days I don't have band, I have to rush to Books and Breads to work. I barely have a social life!" Bastian huffed.

Donnie winced as it dawned on him that his son's high school experience mirrored Susan's. He'd inadvertently fallen into being a strict and controlling parent. Did he want Bastian to head off to college and stay away for the next twenty years? Did he only want his son to come home when decades had passed and he was unable to care for himself anymore?

This moment was his wake-up call. He could continue to order his son around or he could make a change. He took a deep breath. Donnie knew what both Maggie and Susan would say—stop trying to prevent bad things from happening and let people make their own decisions.

"Son, we make a good team. I'm ready to work on communicating with you instead of telling you what to do—for the most part. But I need you to talk to me as well. Let me know when I'm suffocating you. I just want you to be safe and have the best life possible. I'm willing to give you more freedom if you're willing to always be honest with me about where you're going and with whom."

Bastian's face brightened. He pushed his hair back from his face. "If it means you'll sign the paper so I can do driver's ed next month, you can put a tracker on my phone!"

Donnie's eyes widened. "I'm surprised to hear you say that."

"I want you to know how serious I am about driving."

"In that case, I'll take you up on it. For now, you let me have a tracker on your phone until the school year ends. Then we'll go from there."

Bastian stuck out his hand. "Deal."

"But you're still grounded for a month. And you need to pay for any repairs to Jasper's car. And I need to hear you apologize to Eddie. You could have gotten him into a world of trouble."

"I'll be done being grounded by Christmas break?"

Donnie nodded.

Bastian swung his legs off the bed, so he was sitting next to his father. "I hate to admit, you've been very cool about this."

"I don't want to be your warden."

"What's that mean?" Bastian asked.

"I don't want you to feel like a prisoner. I want you to enjoy high school."

"Oh, got it."

"I'll do my best to work on listening to you more, and I need you to understand why I worry."

Bastian smiled and bumped shoulders with his dad. "I get it. I'm all you got."

"Exactly, buddy," Donnie said.

But he thought maybe their family could expand and let in one wonderful, brown-eyed woman. Now all he needed to do was convince her to give him another chance.

Chapter Twenty-Six

♥

Susan

Susan ended the call. She'd been dreading the call since the moment she'd gotten the voicemail. She was glad the conversation with the district superintendent hadn't been awkward. In fact, by the end of the call, they'd been discussing how the school district, especially at the junior high level, could help support her program.

A shiver ran through her. She was really going to do this! She was going to help seniors make friends and find community! The Illinois Department of Aging website was a starting point to look for any programs that were already in place. Perhaps she could replicate something in Marley Creek. Susan frowned. From what she could see, the programs on the website were centered on people who could no longer live on their own. Susan was grateful that the state had options to make it less likely at-risk people would fall through the cracks. It was bittersweet to learn there were programs that could have helped her mom retrofit the house, and maybe she could have avoided falling.

Her research confirmed there wasn't anything in place for older folks that focused on their social and emotional well-being. She was filled with energy, and she started a spreadsheet of potential grant opportunities. Maybe she could even get corporate funding. Susan had spent yesterday on social media and the internet looking for activities for seniors at local park districts and churches, and she'd been disappointed by how few options were available. There were two bingo nights and Marley Creek Recreation had weekly chair yoga, but that was it.

If she could find funding to open a community center, she could offer weekly coffee and pastries. Her heart clenched. Pastries made her think of Donnie. She missed his sad, dark eyes and the way she felt grounded every time he wrapped his arms around her. If things had worked out, she knew he'd be cheering her on. If only he'd given her the respect she deserved.

Now was not the time to get distracted by that brawny man and his mouthwatering brownies. Her stomach fluttered. It would be hard, but she'd need all the help she could get from the business community of Marley Creek. At some point, she was going to have to ask Donnie to help promote her center and cut her a great deal on pastries, bagels, and coffee. If her mother, the queen of deprivation eating, could be drawn in with free food, then Susan should be able to quickly build a clientele. It was just a matter of funding and getting the word out. Thankfully, she had Mayor Belmont on her side.

Susan pulled out her phone to send a text to the group chat and saw a notification from the Concert Buddy app. She hadn't gotten any notifications since the Eliza Fitzsimmons concert. It had only been a couple of months, but Susan felt like she'd been a different person then. The concert might as well have been a couple of years ago. She read the notification; she'd been sent an offer to attend an event. That was weird. She ignored it and sent her text.

Susan got up from the kitchen table to refill her glass of water. She sat back down at her computer and went back to researching how to open her community center. What would be a good name? The Marley Creek Community Center for the Elderly was descriptive but too long, and her mom had a good point, the people she wanted to support weren't going to appreciate being called elderly.

She wanted a name that would draw people in and make them feel part of something. That was the whole point of the center—to catch those people who had faded away from the community and bring them back in, to let them know they weren't alone. Susan spent the next hour working on potential names. A timer went off on her phone, reminding her to make sure Dorothy took her afternoon medication. Susan got up to go to the living room, and she saw the Concert Buddy app notification again. This time, she swiped it open and read. She immediately sat back down. She blinked her eyes, unable to process what she'd read.

Offer: Turkey Bowl

Details: One evening with someone who made a terrible mistake and would like to apologize in front of the entire town.

What you need to do: Respond on Friday.

Additional Comments:

I hope that you'll let me try to make amends. I miss you.

Susan read and re-read the invitation. Her first instinct was to say no, and she knew that was a knee-jerk reaction. She'd gone with her first instinct before and that didn't serve her well at all. She needed to think about this, and more to the point, she needed to talk this over with her friends. Susan fired off a few lines to the group text.

SUSAN: Love life emergency, anyone able to video chat?

NICOLE: Ooooo I'm free after five.

ZAINA: Are you going to get back together with Donnie?!!

SUSAN: Can you talk at five-thirty, Z?

ZAINA: Sure!

DEVIN: It's tight but add me to the call and I'll try to pop on. I do love a love emergency. So much better than a mayor emergency.

Zaina, Nicole, and Susan all liked Devin's text.

SUSAN: Thanks guys, I'll call you all later.

Susan's stomach flip-flopped. She'd been trying so hard to focus on a plan for her center, and it had helped turn her sadness over Donnie into something productive. Maybe she could have Donnie and a new career. What would that be like?

At five-thirty, Susan Face Timed her friends, and even Devin was available to chat.

"Girls, I got an offer on Concert Buddy." Susan said.

"What's it for?" Nicole said.

"More like who's it from?" Asked Zaina.

"Please tell us it's from Donnie." Devin said.

Susan couldn't help but smile. "Yes, Donnie sent me an offer via the app to go to the Turkey Bowl."

"I'm not going to lie—I kind of love that." Zaina said.

"Same here," Nicole said.

"What do you think, Susan? Are you going to say yes?" Devin asked.

"I must admit I'm going back and forth between saying yes, if only to hear him out, and declining the offer all together. When I think about how we left things, I realize I didn't give him much of a chance to explain himself. Then again, he texted me right after the hayride and just said he was sorry I was upset."

"Ugh, I hate the non-apology apology." Nicole said.

"So annoying," Zaina agreed.

"What do you think, Devin?" Susan asked. She didn't know Devin as well as Zaina and Nicole, but she valued Devin's opinions. She felt her temperament aligned most with Devin's.

"My suggestion is to ask yourself which option gives you the least regrets. If saying no means, you'll always wonder what would have happened if you went to the Turkey Bowl. Then you should go."

"Devin, you are brilliant!" said Zaina.

Nicole nodded.

Susan pushed her hair behind her ears. "I'm going to accept his offer. Devin, your advice is perfect. I'd have major regrets if I don't go."

"Virtual group hug, ladies! We've solved another love-life emergency!" Zaina said.

All four of the girls mimed hugging each other. And then Nicole said, "This came about in the most twisty of ways, but yay! Susan's going to the twentieth class reunion!"

Chapter Twenty-Seven

♥

Donnie

Donnie checked the Concert Buddies app again, just to make sure he'd read it correctly. There it was on the screen. Susan had accepted his offer. He'd almost given up hope, and then last night he'd gotten the notification. She was in. He was so nervous; he could hardly take a full breath. It was time to put it all out there and see if she'd take him back. Step one was complete. She was willing to see him again! Now he had to show her he'd changed. He called Bastian into the kitchen to talk over pancakes.

"So, what do you think?" Donnie asked Bastian.

"Susan seems okay. She wanted you to sign the paper for driver's ed. I definitely liked that about her."

"When did she say that?" Donnie asked.

Bastian shrugged. "That time you made her dinner. I heard you two talking. She said that you should let me do the student driving class at school, that I was responsible, and it was probably safer if I learned at school, something like that."

"She was not wrong there. I should have listened to her," Donnie admitted.

"If you are looking for my permission or something, I'm all for you and Susan. She seems cool and I think she's smarter about how to deal with a teenager than you are. She's a psychologist, right?"

"She has a degree in psychology."

"Right, whatever. I bet she'd say it was better for my development if I was able to hang out with friends this week and not still be grounded."

"Tell you what, I'll run that past her, provided we get back together."

Bastian put down his phone and actually looked at his father. "Dad, you're a great guy. I think once you talk to her and show her how much you care and want to make things right, she'll give you another chance. Just make sure you don't screw it up."

"Sage advice from the sophomore."

Bastian unleashed a rare smile. "We're going to blow her away with the halftime show."

"And that is all thanks to you. I'm so grateful you came up with the idea. Can I give you a hug?" Donnie asked.

Bastian shrugged. Donnie walked over and gave his son a squeeze. He couldn't remember the last time he'd hugged his son. That was on him. He should have worked harder to understand why Bastian had been shutting him out. Donnie had been acting more like a guard than a parent. That was changing now. Between Susan dumping him and Bastian getting into a car accident, things had clarified, and Donnie was working on what mattered in his life.

***

Donnie walked along the back of Marley Creek High School. The days were short now that the clocks had been set back for Daylight Savings Time; it was four-fifteen, and the sun was setting. He caught his reflection in the windows and he didn't look away. He saw joy on his face. For once, his smile met his eyes. And he appreciated his tall, broad profile. Sure he had a belly, but darn it if it didn't suit him. Hoping it would bring him good luck, He was wearing the same outfit he'd worn when he met Susan. He knew she'd recognize it. He grinned. *This was a solid plan.*

The parking lot was filling up with alumni. This year the twentieth reunion folks were all wearing orange 'Class of 2004' shirts. He scanned the parking lot for Jasper's car. Susan was driving with Jasper and Zaina. He checked his phone to see if Jasper had texted to let him know they'd arrived. If all went well, Susan would be coming home with him tonight.

As soon as Donnie put his phone back in his pocket, it buzzed. Donnie took it back out and read the text from Jasper that simply said *here.*

Donnie walked to the entrance gate. His heart was racing. He'd missed her so much. He knew that as soon as he saw her, he'd want to give her a bear hug and maybe never let her go. But that was the last thing he should do. He needed to hang back and follow her cues. A small burst of pride went through him;

he was getting better at making it past his smothering instinct. Donnie rocked from foot to foot anxiously, scrutinizing each person as they came close. There were so many women wearing the twentieth reunion shirts. It looked like the entire class of two-thousand and four was in attendance. He was so intent on trying to find Susan that he almost missed it when Zaina, big belly and all, came into view. She'd skipped wearing the class shirt.

Jasper waved his hand and Donnie waved back. His eyes weren't on Jasper, though. He stared unabashedly at Susan, who was talking to Zaina. They were both laughing. Donnie strained his ears to hear the lilt of Susan's laugh over the din of the crowd. And there it was. He couldn't keep the big grin off his face. She turned away from Zaina, and her hair swished over her shoulders. His dick hardened and his chest tightened. He walked toward the three of them. Susan raised her hand in greeting. She had a lopsided smile on her face, and he wanted to kiss the corner of her lips.

"Hi," she said.

"Thanks for coming," he said, and his voice cracked. He held out his hand, hoping she'd take it in hers. Donnie could feel Jasper and Zaina looking on, but he ignored them and held his breath. His palm was sweaty.

Chapter Twenty-Eight

♥

Susan

Susan reached out and took Donnie's hand. She was blown away by how right it felt—his hand in hers—even though both their hands were clammy with nervousness.

"You look cute," he said.

Susan scoffed. "In bright orange?"

Donnie nodded. "You make it look sexy." He squeezed her hand. He handed over their tickets and they got their hands stamped. "Do you want to sit by Jasper and Zaina?"

"Let's ditch the old married folks."

"All right," Donnie said. He led the way up the bleachers and found a section where there weren't many people around. He took off his knapsack, pulled out a blanket, and set it down on the seat. Then got out a second one and wrapped it around Susan.

"This is so thoughtful," she said.

Donnie pulled out a large thermos, a couple of small plastic cups, and a big brownie wrapped in parchment paper.

"Please tell me that's one of your rare dark chocolate orange brownies."

Donnie grinned. "I almost brought s'mores brownies, but then I thought of how your perfume smells like orange blossoms and I brought this."

Susan took his hand and looked into his eyes. "You're very thoughtful and considerate. And I love that about you. Thinking about it, that's part of why I got so upset when I found out you contacted James O'Brien after I asked you not to make decisions for me."

Donnie hung his head, "I'm sorry. Thanks again for coming here tonight."

"I almost didn't," Susan said.

Donnie reached over and Susan took his hand. She wasn't sure where this was going, but she had a delicious brownie and a hot chai to drink. Zaina waved at her from a few rows away. Susan gave her a thumbs up, but inside she was wondering if that was all Donnie was going to say. If that was it, they could have just texted or she could have stopped at Books and Breads.

Because this was the alumni class reunion game, the teams played flag football instead of tackle and the quarters were eight minutes instead of fifteen.

"Jasper said even though it was flag football, he still wasn't going to play. He said he couldn't risk an injury, since Zaina is due in a couple of weeks," Susan said.

"That's smart," Donnie said. He checked his phone and then looked back at her. "I, ah, need to go take care of something. I'll be back in a few minutes, okay?"

Susan frowned. "I guess."

"Great!" he said and stood up quickly, making his way to the aisle and down the bleachers.

Susan followed him with her eyes as he rushed down. He exited the bleachers and walked toward the concession stand. Maybe he had a bathroom emergency.

Nicole walked up the bleachers and sat down next to Susan. "How's it going so far?"

"Fine, I guess? Donnie said he had to take care of something. So far I'm not sure why he wanted me to come here with him."

The halftime buzzer sounded, and the teams walked off the field.

"I'm sorry this isn't going better," Nicole said.

"Wait, what's that?" Susan said. The marching band began walking onto the field. Everyone began clapping as the band started playing, but it wasn't the Marley Creek Fight Song. Susan tilted her head and Nicole grabbed her arm.

The band was playing her favorite Eliza Fitzsimmons song, "Right On Time." The hair on her arms stood up. She began singing along with the lyrics. "I didn't get the job, I did get the speeding ticket, you came along right on time." The band filed onto the field and got into formation as they hit the chorus of the song. Susan was singing at the top of her lungs.

Susan looked around and saw that everyone in the stands was on their feet, even Zaina. The last notes of the song faded away, and the band stood at attention. A voice crackled on the loudspeaker. It was Donnie.

"A few weeks ago, I made a terrible mistake. I was trying to fix something instead of listening to the woman I love."

A lump formed in Susan's throat. The field was starting to swim as her eyes filled with tears. She brushed them away and Donnie continued to speak.

"Susan, it took you dumping me and a car accident to knock some sense into me. I realize now that I was trying so hard to stop bad things from happening that I only wound up hurting the people I love. I love you and I want to build a life with you—and Bastain and Dorothy too!"

Susan hugged herself and Nicole put her arm around Susan's shoulders. "What do you think?" Nicole whispered to Susan.

Susan put her hands up to her mouth and shouted, "I think you're 'Right On Time,' Donnie!" The crowd erupted into cheers and the band started playing Eliza Fitzsimmons's viral hit 'Let's Make This Forever.'

Donnie made a heart with his hands and walked off the field and back into the stands. Nicole gave Susan one last squeeze and exited the row to make room for Donnie.

Donnie stood next to Susan. His brown eyes weren't sad, now they were hopeful. She threw her arms around him and kissed him like her life depended on it. When they came up for air, Donnie asked. "Will you go steady with me?"

"Steady? I thought you wanted to marry me?" Susan said, half-joking.

"Heck, I'll marry you tonight at the reunion dance. I heard Father Edward was going to be there. He's class of two-thousand and four."

"So, what I'm hearing is that we are engaged."

"W-will you marry me, Susan?"

Susan took Donnie's hand, "It's so funny that an app brought us together. You know, we are always going to have to explain it wasn't one of 'those' apps."

Donnie chuckled nervously. "But?"

Susan caressed his hand, "But I wouldn't change any of this. Yes, I will marry you, Donnie Larson—but not tonight. Tonight is for making out under the bleachers and then dancing until the cows come home."

<h1 style="text-align:center;font-style:italic">Epilogue</h1>

♥

Donnie

Bastian had his driver's license for a year now, but Donnie still worried. He hadn't had any panic attacks in that time, so that was a win. He waved as his son drove off to start his senior year of high school. The new porch swing beckoned, so he sat down and pushed off with his feet. Maggie and Donnie had started a tradition of Bastian's first day of school breakfast when he'd started kindergarten. She'd only gotten to be there for that first year and as hard as it was, Donnie had kept the tradition alive. And now his son was starting his last year of school.

He was going to be a mess when graduation rolled around. But unlike those earlier years, he wasn't alone anymore. Donnie had Susan—and not only that, he'd also gained a mother-in-law who'd helped him make first-day-of-school chocolate chip banana pancakes this morning.

Even better, this evening was the official grand opening of Owl House. It was a day of celebration for the Brown-Larson family. The front door swung open, and he smelled fresh coffee.

"How are you doing out here?" Susan said.

Donnie looked over at his bride. She was radiant this morning in her simple white T-shirt and cutoff jean shorts. She was holding two coffee cups; she handed him the one that had *Mr.* in script on it and kept the *Mrs.* cup for herself.

"When you're near, I'm always good." He patted the wooden slats of the swing. "Come sit next to me." She sat down next to him and he wrapped his free arm around her. "I hope your mom isn't inside doing the dishes."

Susan smiled. "I talked her out of washing them by hand, but she insisted on loading the dishwasher."

Donnie took a sip of his coffee. "Coffee just tastes better when you have the luxury of sitting outside on a late summer morning with your wife."

Susan put out her hand and looked at her still-new wedding ring. "Have I told you how lucky I am to be married to the best baker in Marley Creek?"

Donnie tickled Susan's side until she squirmed. "Hey," he said and waggled his eyebrows. "What time is your mom leaving for physical therapy?"

Susan checked her watch. "Very soon."

"Do you have any last-minute to-dos for the grand opening, or...?" He winked at her.

"That depends. Do you have time to help me over at Owl House this afternoon?"

"I'm all yours."

"Then I'm all yours as soon as my mom leaves."

Donnie put down his coffee mug and pulled Susan onto his lap.

She gasped in surprise. "Mr. Larson!"

He kissed her neck. "I can't wait to take you upstairs and pull off those jeans." As he spoke, he discreetly slid his hand under the frayed edge of her cutoffs. His hands caressed the silky soft skin of her thigh.

A Prius pulled up in front of the house. Susan climbed off his lap, and he almost groaned at the loss of her sweet ass against his hardened cock. He pulled a cushion over his lap. Susan opened the front door. "Mom, your ride is here!"

"Let them know I'll be out in a minute," Dorothy said from the living room.

"Hon, can you tell the driver to pull up in the driveway?"

Donnie made himself think about the monthly sale taxes he needed to submit this week for Books and Breads. His libido came to a screeching halt. He walked across the lawn and told the driver to pull up into the driveway. By the time he was back on the porch, Susan was following her mom out to the car. Donnie noticed Dorothy balancing so well she barely needed her cane. Still, he was glad she wasn't so stubborn as to try to go out without it. Soon the Prius was pulling out of the driveway.

Donnie abandoned his coffee to chase Susan as she ran into the house. He followed her through the living room and almost tripped over an ottoman because he was so distracted by a peek of her cheeks through the fringe of her cutoffs.

"Damn, woman!" he growled.

Susan's laugh floated down the hall as she ducked into their bedroom. He came into the room and paused for a moment. Susan stripped off her clothes. Tossing her T-shirt and jean shorts on the floor, all she had on was a pair of black bikini panties. He'd never even dared to hope after Maggie died that he'd find love like this again. His heart filled his chest, and he thanked Maggie for the joy. He'd done the same on his wedding day. She would always be his North Star. He liked to think that somewhere beyond this earth, Maggie had sent Susan his way to help him from being alone once Bastian was grown.

Donnie shook himself from his musings.

"What are you waiting for?" Susan shimmied on the bed. Donnie carefully dove onto the bed next to Susan and then he rolled on top of her. Holding himself on his elbows, he leaned down, taking her bottom lip between his teeth. She kissed him back.

He kissed the special spot just under her ear, where he'd given her a hickey back when they'd made out in the high school theater. Warmth flooded his abdomen as the memory of that night mingled with the soft press of her body beneath his.

"What are you thinking about?" She asked.

"How fucking lucky I am to have you as my wife."

Susan wrapped her legs around his waist. Her wet pussy pressed against his dick. He could smell the honeyed scent of her juices. His mouth watered. He hooked his finger into the top of her panties and pulled them off as he backed down her soft body. He kissed the inside of her knee and then slid the panties all the way off.

She lay in front of him, her eyes closed, and her knees bent. He caressed her calves, delighting in the shiver that ran through her. She let her legs fall open and Donnie began kissing his way to her glistening pussy. He nestled his head between her voluptuous thighs and swiped his tongue through her folds. He practically slurped her as he wound his way around her clit. She grabbed a handful of his hair, and he responded by sucking lightly on her swollen nub.

"Yes, Donnie, just like that."

He took her words to heart and repeated the motions until her legs were shaking and she was writhing on the bed. She bucked against his mouth. He pushed two fingers into her and curved them, working to find her g-spot. He sped up his motions, diving to catch every drop of her in his mouth.

"Yes! Oh My God! Yes!" she shouted as she came. Her shouts drove him wild, and he rutted against the bed. Would he be able to hold off his own climax, or was he going to spill all over this bed like he was seventeen instead of forty-seven? He grinned against her pussy. He savored every moment with her. To think he'd almost missed it all.

***

Susan looked down at Donnie who was propped up on his elbows gazing at her. The corners of his lips turned up, and she watched as he licked her off his lips. She reached down and caressed his cheek.

"My turn," she said.

"How do you want to do it?"

"Lie back and let me show you." She winked.

He moved next to her on his back. Pride swelled within her as she looked down at his throbbing cock. Wrapping her hands around it, she focused on enjoying the smooth feel of his skin. She started off by licking the prominent veins from root to stem. Then she put her mouth on his cock, swirling the precum off the tip, and down the shaft as she moved down, down, and then finally he was butting against the back of her throat. Her eyes watered and she backed off.

She slowly released him, replacing her mouth with her hand and stroking him anew. She gasped. Donnie curled his hand around her boob and began teasing her swollen nipple with his thumb, sliding and tweaking as she moved to put his balls in her mouth. They were nearly as hard as his cock, and she knew he was close to coming already. Susan ran her tongue over his balls, enjoying the way he was rocking back and forth into her touch on his cock and her mouth down below.

"Sugar," he gasped.

"Mmmmm," she replied.

"I can't take anymore. I need that tight pussy of yours."

His words went straight to her core. She took her hand off his cock and touched herself. Her fingers slid through her wetness as she rubbed her clit.

Donnie looked down at her. "God, you're so fucking hot when you do that."

Susan straddled him. "I love how powerful you make me feel." She lined up against his dick, sliding slowly against it. Looking at Donnie, the lust in his eyes turned her on even more. He placed his hands on her hips and looked at her, his eyebrow raised.

Susan nodded, and Donnie lifted her up. She gripped his cock and angled herself. She slowly pushed herself down, enjoying the fullness. When she had him inside her, she ground down. Then she rode him, chasing her own release and pushing him toward his. The euphoria built, and she tried to hold on a little longer, but it felt too good.

"Yes, Susan! You're so tight! Yes!" Donnie shouted.

She melted as he grabbed her ass. God, she loved the strength and size of him.

The headboard rocked against the wall as they came together. Susan collapsed on top of him, and Donnie ran his hands up and down her back. She inhaled the smell of them mixing together. A summer breeze fluttered the curtains, wafting over them and cooling her heated skin.

"Shit, I hope Mrs. Mckindley isn't outside in the garden this morning." Susan blushed.

Donnie chuckled, and the hair on his chest tickled her. "Thank you for this."

"Why are you thanking me? I love having sex with you. Your sexual prowess is why I married you."

Donnie grinned. "Because you have the grand opening of Owl House tonight."

"Aww, that is really sweet of you to be thinking about my career."

"My life's goal is to be your biggest cheerleader," he said. Susan's heart swelled. She kissed Donnie's forehead, then his cheeks, and finally moved over to his full lips. She kissed him slowly. He teased the seam of her lips with his tongue, and she let him in for a moment. Then she pulled back and rolled off him.

"I'm so excited! What a great way to start this day. Thank you, baby."

Donnie caressed her cheek. "I won't even distract you by offering to wash your back."

"Rain check on that?"

Donnie grinned. The adoration in his eyes took her breath away.

"Damn, I'm a lucky girl." She said.

"I'm the lucky one," Donnie countered.

***

Donnie fussed with the dessert table. He moved the brownie bites closer to the front, so no one would have trouble reaching them, and added another set of mini tongs. There was a tiered tray of mini cupcakes: chocolate, vanilla, and carrot cake. Susan, Bastian, and Donnie had a bet as to which of the cupcakes would be gone first. Donnie's money was on carrot cake.

Donnie chuckled. When he won, Susan and Bastian would have to spend a Saturday watching the three *Lord of The Rings* movies, director's cut, with him. Warmth suffused his chest. If you would have told him two years ago not only would he find love again, but that he'd have two strong women to help him navigate Bastian's rocky teen years? He wouldn't have believed it.

The scent of orange blossom and vanilla preceded a gentle poke in his side. "Boo!" Susan said. She was dressed in blue slacks, a T-shirt emblazoned with the Owl House logo, and a cardigan. Her long brown hair was up in a bun. He wrapped his arm around her.

"You're incredible, you know that?" he asked.

"No one has shown up yet. Let's wait and see how this goes today."

"You've already saved your mom, and me too, from loneliness. It's going to be even easier to do that with strangers."

The corners of Susan's lips turned up. "You say some of the wisest things. Are you sure you didn't get a degree in sociology? Psychology?"

Donnie shook his head. "My keen insight into human nature is due to hours and hours watching people. You can tell a lot about people based on their coffee, pastry, and book choices."

Susan put her hand in Donnie's. He felt the cool sweat of her palm. He kissed her head. "You've got this. Look, here comes Jasper and Zaina." Donnie pointed at the couple who were walking up the sidewalk. Just behind them was an older woman. Jasper entered first, holding the door for Zaina and the woman.

Susan and Donnie walked over. Zaina looked around and then threw her arms around Susan. "I'm so proud of you! This place looks amazing!"

Donnie was beginning to wonder if his face would freeze into a permanent grin. He loved seeing his wife getting all the attention and adoration she deserved. She'd worked so hard to get this place off the ground so she could make life better for the isolated elders of Marley Creek.

"Susan, I'd like to introduce my mother to you," Jasper said. Donnie watched as Susan greeted Jasper's mother and then walked her over to meet Dorothy. Donnie raised an eyebrow at Jasper, who sidled up to him and whispered. "I called her on a whim, sure she was going to say no, but she wanted to come."

Donnie rocked on his heels. "I'm so damn excited for Susan and for everyone who's going to start coming here."

More guests began to stream into Owl House and soon the room was filled with friends, local business owners, and more senior residents than Donnie had ever seen in one place in Marley Creek. He stood to the side as Susan spoke into the microphone. Susan thanked everyone for their support and for coming to the grand opening. Then she looked over at Donnie, and he started blinking back tears.

"Lastly, thank you, Donnie. You are my biggest cheerleader. Like Eliza Fitzsimmons says, 'Without the silence of your love, no one could hear me sing.'"

Donnie blew his love a kiss.

***

Ready for another visit to Marley Creek? Pre-order Brandee and Luc's story: ***Your Mr. Brightside https://a.co/d/bPsO85o***

Susan's Soup Recipe

Here is the full recipe for the soup Susan makes for her mom.
Enjoy!

Butternut-Leek Soup

Ingredients:

One Butternut Squash, peeled and diced

Slice two leeks, just the white and a little of the light green
portion.

Peel and dice one potato or sweet potato

Peel and slice one parsnip. (optional, this is my secret
ingredient)

4-5 cups of vegetable or chicken (if you don't need it to be
vegetarian) broth

a tbsp of dried poultry seasoning or thyme

or 1-2 tbsps fresh rosemary and thyme

Salt and pepper to taste.

Put it all in a slow cooker on low and cook for 6-8 hours or
until the vegetables are soft. Then use an immersion blender to
puree the soup. Serve with gruyere or Swiss cheese grated on top
or add a couple of tbsps of diced ham or crumbled bacon. This

soup pairs very well with a nice crusty bread. I would pair it with a Reisling or glass of Chardonnay. The leftovers taste great and this soup freezes well. If you try it let me know!

Also By Victoria Hamel

♥

Book One in the Marley Creek Romance Series; *No Gouda Without You*

Get your copy of book one here:
https://a.co/d/jeeF06E

Book Two in the Marley Creek Romance Series: *Too Kölsch For Comfort*

**Get your copy of book two here:
https://a.co/d/0avDaHZ**

**Book Three in the Marley Creek Romance Series:
*Is This Love Fur Real?***

Get your copy here: https://a.co/d/fEIOZJx

**Book Four in the Marley Creek Romance Series: *It
App-ened One Night***

Get your copy here: https://a.co/d/5qpVaaj

**Book Five in the Marley Creek Romance Series:
*Your Mr. Brightside***

**Pre-order your copy here:
https://a.co/d/h1TWrEV**

Sign up for Victoria's free newsletter for sneak peeks, special offers and more by visiting her website https://victoriahamelauthor.com

About the Author

♥

Victoria's love of writing began in grade school where she won an award for a Mother's Day essay. She spent the better part of her childhood with her head in a book. In high school, she wrote love stories for her friends in which they'd meet their favorite bands or the movie star they had a crush on. Suffice it to say, Victoria was writing fan fiction before fan fiction was a thing. After spending many years starting and stopping writing in various genres, Victoria returned to her high school roots and began writing romance.

Victoria Hamel lives in the Chicago area with her husband, three college-age kids and Bowie the dog. She has run three marathons and based on that experience; she feels qualified to say that reviewing her manuscript for errors was a more arduous task than literally running a marathon. She is a member of the Chicago North Romance Writers Group as well as Contemporary Romance Writers. When she isn't writing, Victoria volunteers for local democrat candidates, watches K-Dramas, or can be found blogging on her blog *First of All...*

You can find the other books in the Marley Creek Romance series here or via any independent bookstore:

https://www.amazon.com/stores/author/B0CSBGDRFQ

Subscribe to my newsletter for exclusive bonus scenes, ARC opportunities, and all the news!